Hoovering the Roof 2

An anthology of work from the East Dulwich Writers' Group

London, UK

Cover and illustrations by RHKW
Printed by - lightning source.

This book is dedicated to the friends and families
of all the contributors.

earwig press

Introduction

A year has past since *Hoovering the Roof*, the first anthology from the East Dulwich Writers' Group, made its fledgling appearance. In that time, we have continued to do all the things we do so well: drinking tea, eating biscuits, talking, writing, reading, and critiquing each other's work.

The first edition of *Hoovering the Roof* disappeared off the shelves in record time and was the runner-up in The National Association of Writers' Groups' Annual Writing Awards 2010, for the best anthology by a writing group - all of which made us even more intent on delivering the finest writing we could for this second collection.

For this new anthology, titled, yes, *Hoovering the Roof 2*, we have once again worked hard to produce thought- provoking stories, engaging poems and controversial social satire. Our membership has grown with our success, and we remain open to new talent while continuing to nurture our existing writers.

We have people at every stage of their writing careers - from absolute beginners, to published authors and competition winners.

Heart-warmingly, the octogenarians still turn up, despite the hills, to share their inimitable sense of style. The younger ones bring with them their enthusiasm and willingness to make mistakes. Those in the middle strike a balance between the two, and try not to hog all the biscuits. May our tribe increase.

Learn more about EDWG, and comment on both our anthologies at our website: www.edwg.co.uk and on Facebook

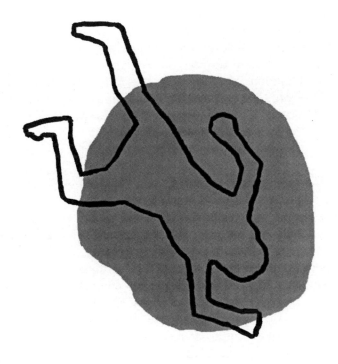

Contents

Contents

Contents

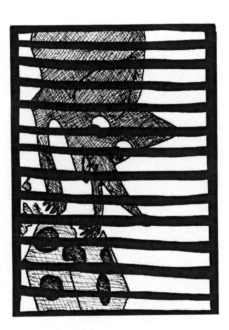

Of Mice and Mistletoe

FABIAN ACKER

I've finally trained him! *All I have to do is jump into this little wheel, take a few turns round and he pushes a piece of cheese through the slot.*

He's quite bright really, for a scientist. When I first came here, he used to drop in nuts and seeds occasionally, but it was more or less at random. But, you see, I know a thing or two about scientists. I mean, I ought to by now. I was born in these labs, and I've seen them every day all my life. There's something about a little wheel that really excites them. You just have take a turn or two, and they start jabbering to each other, and it's easy to condition them after that.

Fundamentally, scientists are very anxious, and because of that, eager to please. I just have to squeak five or six time in a row, and one of them will come running. They're really very sweet.

I prefer squeaking when one of the females is about; the males don't engage properly. They check the cage, the water, the litter tray, but they never really look at you. Look, see that female over there — she's one of the best. When she's alone, she comes over to me as soon as I squeak and she'll put her finger in and stroke me. It smells of some sort of flower, I think. I've never seen one, but my grandpa used to be in the field before he volunteered to help out here, and he told me about them and how they smell.

1

Actually I'm a bit worried about her. This last week she's been behaving quite out of character. When she sees that she's alone, she gets up on one of the chairs, and hangs a kind of whitish berry from the ceiling. There are three of them up already. If it had to do with some experiment with us, she wouldn't wait 'til no one's about. They'd discuss it all hours and then they'd do an experiment. But look! She's doing it now.

She's also putting coloured paper on the walls, and pictures of an old man with a white beard. Could be her Dad, or maybe a leading scientist. He doesn't look very bright, but that's not unusual for a scientist.

She'd better be quick. My whiskers tell me the boss is on his way, but she can't sense him yet. Those whiskers under her nose are so short they're almost invisible. They're bloody useless. Probably more of an embarrassment than a sensor.

Whup! There she goes! She's heard him. Down from the chair, starting to stare intently at a cage - been empty for a month that one - and look; she's putting some red stuff on her lips. Antiseptic I suppose. And some antibiotic behind her ears. Won't do any good, Miss. Has to be injected. I've been here long enough to know that

He's quite a nice chap, her boss. Thick as a guinea pig, but amiable and always quick with the cheese when I trigger him. I just wish he'd give up on that low-cholesterol crap. I might have to condition him a bit more, to see if he can distinguish between that and Gorgonzola.

See what I mean about being thick? He's talking to the female now, but not actually looking at her. You might think he's talking to one of the mice in the Larchmead Estate over in Complex B.

'You see, Miss Fotheringay, it's a simple conditioned reflex. When he first came into the cage some weeks ago, every time I saw him running in the wheel, I dropped a piece of cheese in the slot. In his little mouse mind, he associates cheese with wheel. Cheese and wheel, wheel and cheese. Classical association.'

(And every time I see you, Miss Fotheringay, I associate you with sex. Strictly speaking it's not a conditioned reflex — yet — because I haven't been rewarded for my intention, except in my mind, but every time I see you I want to unbutton your white coat and hug you tight and kiss you. Would you despise me for that? Yes, you would. You're my student, I'm twice your age, and there are so many young and good-looking men in your year. I'd get struck off, and you'd be laughed at. What would *Physics Review* make of that? "Professor ends career with inappropriate fondling. Ignatius Theopholus, leading research worker etc etc." But, oh Miss Fotheringay, it would be worth it.)

'Yes that's quite clear. But, Dr Theopholus, shouldn't you vary the reward? What happens if he gets sated with cheese? *(Now you're bloody talking, woman; I'm not "sated" with cheese, just low-cholesterol cheese)* Nicholas and others found in their paper that with pigeons and mistletoe, I mean pigeons and thistle-mow, what am I thinking? With pigeons and thistle-mow, the reflex weakened if they were constantly rewarded with, er, just thistle-mow.'

(I'm talking absolute gibberish. 'Thistle-mow'? Never heard of it. Stuff left over when you mow a thistle? I can't possibly get a pass mark this year. Every time I see him, my knees go weak and my pulse quickens. Ignatius, can't you see how much I love you? Why don't you look at me instead of all those cages and mice? If you would just look into my eyes, all this talk about conditioning would disappear. Look at them! Or if you're too shy, look up there, look at the ceiling instead, you lovely silly man. I'm talking mistletoe, you know, not thistle-mow.)

'No, I haven't read that paper, unfortunately, and — oh, what are you looking at? What's that stuck on the ceiling over there? It looks like the larvae of the lesser *cphemeropta pylometra*. How curious. I must look more closely. Have you seen my glasses anywhere, Miss Fotheringay?'

Those two! You could squeak 'til your bladder burst. What about all that conditioning I've done on them? Why don't they listen to me? Look, both of you. See, I'm on the wheel. I'm exhausted. I don't care what kind of cheese it is. Just slip it in. Why are they getting so red? They're breathing as if they've been on the wheel for an hour, and still they won't listen to me. I think I might have to discard them and get another pair. Send them back to the field.

'They're in your breast pocket, Dr Theopholus.' (Oh God, I wish they were in mine.) And they're not pupae. I believe it's called mistletoe. Something to do with Christmas. Oh goodness me. Of course. It's Christmas Eve today. How these things creep up on one. I ought to say "Merry Christmas", Dr Theopholus.'

'Well so it is. And Merry Christmas to you too. I don't really take much notice of these things. Research you know is like Christmas every day.' (What a load of drivel. Am I saying this?) 'And of course, I see now, yes it's mistletoe. *Viscum album* to give it its proper name. Many useful properties. Antispasmodic, immune stimulant, sedative, vasodilator etc etc.' (And kissing. Oh God. Kissing!) Quite an interesting plant but very unprofessional hung up in a laboratory. And quite pagan too, I must find out who put it there. And discipline her. Or him. I believe it generates a conditioned reflex among the lay staff. Osculation. 'Kissing' they call it. Oh, Miss Fotheringay. You appear quite agitated. How curious. You're standing directly underneath some *viscum*. Is it affecting you? Are you in need of an immune stimulant? Or vasodilation? Here, take my arm. Take a few slow, breaths. Just stay still a moment until you feel a little calmer. You're breathing is a little hyper, Miss Fotheringay. Your rapid breast, er, chest movement suggests CO_2 deficiency.'

Look at me you crapulous specimens! Look! I'm still on the wheel. Call yourself scientists? I've got more science in the tip of my tail than you have between you. What am I saying? There's nothing at all between you. What are they doing? Where's my cheese?

'Oh, Ignatius! Oh. That's wonderful. Merry Christmas, my lovely professor!'

'Ah, Muriel! Merry Christmas, my sweet, sweet student!'

Little Bubbles

DANIEL MAITLAND

Little bubbles,
Tiny faces,
Shining eye,
Convex reflections.
Outside: the whole and
limitless world;
Inside, apparently, nothing.

A Matter of Life After Death

AMY GRIGGS

Meredith awoke with a start, sobbing and shivering, as she had done nearly every night since the accident. Caught in that halfway world between dreams and reality, she turned towards him, waiting for him to pull her into his arms and soothe her as one does a small child.

But Meredith was not a child anymore and John was not there to comfort and protect her, as he had nearly every day of their 10-year marriage. Her hand met with emptiness, the merest hint of a hollow dent where his solid bulk had once lain. So solid, so secure, there had been no warning signs to indicate that one day he would simply cease to exist.

Reality bit afresh and Meredith sobbed into the pillow until it was pulpy between her fingers. Stumbling out of bed, she pulled open the wardrobe door - a walnut piece they had inherited from John's mother - and ran her fingers over his shirts, pulled a sleeve to her cheek. The wardrobe had become something of a shrine for Meredith, the row of crisp shirts idols to revere.

However, although precious as symbols of John, of the pride he took in his appearance, in representing his clients at the firm of Ashton, Ashton & Drake to the very best of his ability, they were just shirts and contained none of his essence.

For that she would go to the right-hand drawer, her own private treasure chest. Inside lay a grey, woollen jumper - the one he had been wearing the last full day they spent together. Closing her eyes, Meredith thought back to that day; it had been nothing out of the ordinary, just a routine Saturday filled with supermarket wrangling, mowing the lawn and a bottle of red over dinner. Yet somehow its very usualness gave it an exquisite aura, encapsulating the intimate foundations of their marriage.

In the months since his death, Meredith had developed a new routine, which was replacing the one she had been hard-wired to perform, synapse by synapse. She would start by turning the wrought iron key in the chest of drawers, fingers trembling. Then she would inch out the top drawer and survey the jumper, sometimes for up to a minute at a time before touching it. Even then she would allow herself only to run her fingertips over it at first. Sometimes, this would be enough and she would jolt the drawer back into place. At other times, she would lift it from its resting place and cradle it to her body, breathing in the smell that was intrinsically John.

Once, she had fallen asleep like this and had awoken in a frenzy, lest his smell had become contaminated with her own. Since then she had been strict with herself - a minute, two minutes maximum, then she must fold and return it, smoothing out the creases with loving care.

Tonight, she knew touching would not be enough. She needed to hold it to her, breathe him in, feel him against her skin. The ancient drawer groaned and grunted as she heaved it open, and then... nothing. It was empty. She stared in disbelief, scrabbling around inside in case her eyes were deceiving her. They were not. The jumper had gone.

Meredith staggered across the room pulling open doors, throwing aside covers, cushions, rugs. It must be here. She always put it back in the drawer - *always*.

Her breathing came and went in staccato rasps. 'Keep calm,' she said to herself. Palms pressed flat down on top of the chest's grainy surface, she took long regulated breaths until her heartbeat slowed.

When had she had it last? Yesterday? The day before? The days tended to blur together. Saturday - that was it, she had been holding it when Zoe came round.

Bent over and huddled into herself like an old woman, she shuffled out onto the landing. At the far end, an antique telephone resided in state, a wedding present from some eccentric cousin.

Hands shaking, she picked up the receiver, dialled the number, listened to the satisfying whir clickety click as each numeral slotted back into place, and waited, cat-like, on her haunches. She felt weightless, suspended in time, caught between one second and the next. The line connected. It rang once, twice, three times…

'Come on, Zoe…'

'Hello?'

'Zoe, it's me.'

'Meredith? Are you okay?'

'Yes I have to ask you something Zoe, I *have* to ask you.' She paused to regroup scattered thoughts. 'There was a jumper when you came over on Saturday, I was holding a grey jumper, do you remember? Now I can't find it, I can't find it.'

'Meredith, it's four in the morning!'

'I know, but I need it Zoe, I need it and I can't find it and I can't remember - after you came, I can't remember anything.'

'Okay Mez, remember what the doctor said - deep breaths right? Try to stay calm. You were pretty out of it on Saturday, Zack and I were really worried about you. I stayed with you all night, till you woke up in the morning - remember we had tea and toast outside. You said…'

'Yes, yes I suppose so - but the jumper…'

'Mez, I don't remember you holding any jumper - wait, I did some washing though, while you were sleeping. There were all these clothes scattered round the house - I know you're going through hell right now, but you really need to start taking care of yourself again, you can't wallow in grief forever. It might sound harsh, but life goes on. Meredith? Are you even listening to me?'

She sighed. 'Anyway, if you dropped the jumper I probably picked it up and washed it with everything else. Have you checked the utility room? *Meredith?*'

But Meredith was already running downstairs, leaving the discarded receiver to dangle and clash against a wrought iron table leg. On the bottom step, she paused, dug her nails into the palms of her hands, squeezed her eyes tight shut.

'Let it not be true, oh God, please let it not be true.' Inching towards the utility room, a screw tightened in her stomach. She hesitated again, counting time in her head, ten seconds passed, twenty. She pushed open the door.

Her eyes scanned the rigid clothes rack, taking in the pair of denims, the cashmere cardigan, the row of sensible M&S underwear (what use had she for black lace now?). Her breathing slowed, her body unclenched and relaxed. It wasn't there.

Then, just as she was turning, a sliver of silver caught her eye; it was the tip of a wire coat hanger.

'Ohhh,' she twisted the rack round, sobbing, clawing at it as a leg got caught in the edge of a tile. The jumper swung back and forth in mocking triumph. Meredith pulled it to her, wrestling it from the hanger, inhaled it, but there was nothing. That precious smell that belonged to him - was him - had been washed away. The last part of John obliterated by Economy 30.

Dropping to her knees, Meredith howled her anguish, over and over again, until sheer, physical exhaustion overtook her and she fell asleep on the floor, cheek to granite, her skeletal frame curled around the jumper as if it was all she had left in the world.

Next door, Meredith's neighbour was making himself a cheese and pickle sandwich in the kitchen, having just returned from a night shift at the hospital. Some people said that cheese gave you nightmares, but Greg had always found it quite soothing - a most misunderstood late-night snack.

Halfway through buttering the second slice of bread, he paused, knife in mid-air, listening to Meredith's cries through the paper-thin walls. This was not the first time Greg had heard her despair and, not a stranger to grief himself, he was overcome with compassion and an overarching desire to reach out to her.

Placing his hand on the wall between them, he let it rest there for a minute or more, caressing it with the yellowed tips of his fingers, as if by doing so he could somehow relieve her pain. But cocooned in her own four walls, Meredith was unreachable, oblivious to everything but her own loss.

Sighing, Greg took his hand away and turned to get the cheese from the fridge.

John paced backwards and forwards in the hallway, or rather he floated backwards and forwards since, in his official capacity as Ghost in Residence, he technically didn't have legs.

This being dead lark certainly wasn't all it was cracked up to be. When the accident had first happened, he'd been cautiously optimistic. Okay, admittedly the situation wasn't ideal, but there were a lot of worse places one could have as an afterlife than the comfort of one's own home. Plenty of opportunity to read all those books he'd been meaning to start for ages, but never quite found the time for. He might even get round to putting up the shelf in the bathroom like he'd been promising Meredith he'd do for a year and a half - that would be a nice surprise for her. And then when she was out, there was all that sport he could watch on TV, always assuming she didn't cancel their Sky subscription, like she'd threatened during the last Ashes series.

Reality, however, had turned out to be somewhat different. For a start, classics he'd collected for a rainy day seemed a lot less appealing now he actually had the time to read them. He'd read pretty much everything else in the bookcase, and who wanted to read a thriller again when you already knew whodunnit?

Then there was the matter of the shelf. All the tools were in the tool shed and, in his current state, John was unable to leave the house. He'd tried it once and the blood rushed from his top to his bottom in such a peculiar manner that he felt disinclined to try again, putting any prospective DIY projects on hold indefinitely. This alone might not have curtailed his enjoyment of the afterlife. After all, he really couldn't be blamed for the continued lack of shelf and could now watch the rugby guilt-free. Or he could if the woman would ever leave the house. But she didn't. Ever.

Instead she wandered from room to room all day, trailing that awful grey sweater around that she'd bought him last Christmas and he'd felt obliged to wear every third month just to prove he liked it. It was just his luck, that of all the pieces of clothing he could be remembered by it would be that one. He didn't even like grey for heaven's sake and the wool was coarse and itchy, especially round the neck.

When Zoe had washed it, he'd been pleased - at least if it lost its significance for her, Meredith might give it a rest, get rid of it even, either by giving it to a charity shop or, best case scenario, burying it in a hole in the garden.

But now he could see how distraught she was, he was filled with remorse. If he was honest, this wasn't exactly an isolated incident. She'd been building up to something like it for a while.

It was, of course, horrible watching someone you love be so upset, but there had been a part of him - the same part that caused him to say 'lookin' good' while standing in front of the mirror every morning - that had been secretly pleased by her grief and the amount she missed him.

Being dead was turning out to be a pretty raw deal, so at the very least he reckoned he deserved a bit of an ego massage. But this was different, this wasn't normal grief, it was bordering on madness. He was seriously worried about her now, Meredith seemed to be losing it, and he hadn't the least idea how to help her.

He'd tried patting her on the shoulder of course, but what body he did have slid right through her in a manner that was disconcerting to him and had no perceivable effect on her. If anything, she'd seemed to wail louder. This in itself was odd. He had no problem taking hold of objects when the need arose, but people, apparently, eluded him. It was a puzzle, but then he supposed if you could do everything in the afterlife that you could in life there'd be no point to the thing at all, and since death seemed to have put a bit of a dampener on his libido, it didn't bother him unduly. Not that this helped the current situation in the slightest.

No, this was a problem that would take some thought, and he hovered above the bottom stair to do just that.

Meredith woke next morning to loud and persistent rapping on the front door. Groaning, she stretched and rolled over. Somewhere during the early hours of the morning, she had made it back upstairs, but had an unpleasant crick in her neck from falling asleep on the floor, not to mention a pounding headache. The jumper lay crushed on the pillow beside her.

Outside, the rapping continued, this time accompanied by the shrill whistle of the bell. Rubbing her eyes, Meredith pulled on her dressing gown - a cream towelling affair - and stumbled downstairs. She opened the door a couple of inches, just as a second whistle penetrated her ear-drums, and peered through the gap, pulling the gown tighter around her.

The man on the doorstep was about mid-forties, a little on the thin side perhaps, but not unattractive, with unruly brown hair and almond eyes. He seemed somewhat familiar to her, yet for a second or two she could not think why. Then he spoke, and she realised it was her neighbour - Jeff? George? Names were not Meredith's strong point at the best of times, let alone after a night on sleeping pills and wine.

'Hi, the postman dropped this in to me. He said he couldn't get an answer when he knocked here before, but I saw a light on so thought you must be in.' His eyes, when she looked into them, expressed a concern that lay unspoken between them.

Meredith opened the door wider, taking in the fact that there was a large cardboard box on the path beside him and also that it might not be as early as she had assumed. Might not be morning even.

'Oh right, thanks, I must have been asleep, I'll take it now.' Their hands collided as both attempted to take ownership of the parcel.

'It's heavy - books I think. Let me carry it in for you.' Meredith hesitated, ran a hand through her tousled hair, worried about her bed-clothed state and the messy rooms behind her. But he already had the box in his arms, and she felt powerless to do anything other than step back and let him in.

'Where should I put it?'

'Um, just there on the table will be fine. I'll move these papers, sorry, it isn't usually so untidy. What a big box! I can't think what it is.' She twisted her fingers. Wished he would go.

'No worries - you should see my living room.' He smiled at her. 'Looks like there's some kind of university logo on the side. You doing a course or something?'

'Oh, oh yes I am - was, I mean,' she said, disorientated both by the recollection and the fact that she had forgotten so completely in the first place.

'What in? Something weighty clearly!'

'Modern history. We went to Russia a couple of years ago and since then I've had a fascination for the Tsars and the Russian Revolution and then I saw this distance learning course advertised...'

'But you changed your mind?'

She stared at him for a second. The question seemed almost non-sensical, it was so far devolved from her present reality. 'Changed my mind? No, I mean it's just that all that was before... um my husband was... my husband was killed in a car accident earlier this year and I've found it quite difficult to... to...' He touched her wrist. She stared at the dark hairs curling around the back of his hand. Found herself counting them.

'Meredith. I'm so sorry. Sit down, what can I do? Let me make you some tea.' She turned her head away, ashamed of being seen like this. He placed a hand on her shoulder and, meeting no resistance, drew her into him. The hint of soap and warm bread, and something else - ginger? - enveloped her. Rain trickled down the window. A clock chimed the hour and ticked on.

At length, she pulled away, awkward and uncertain again. He smiled at her. 'So how about that tea then? Or coffee, I can do that too? A man of many talents.'

She returned the smile, wiping her eyes. 'No, really, thanks, it should be me offering you a cup of tea anyway, but...'

'But you'd rather I left you alone.'

'I'm sorry.'

'Why? You have nothing to be sorry about, as long as you remember I'm only next-door and I keep a fully stocked wine rack, anytime you feel like some company. And I do understand - more than you think. My wife died of cancer five years ago and I would give up everything I have just to hear her voice one more time.'

She looked up at him, surprised by the sudden catch in his voice. She had been too consumed by her own grief to notice anything around her for such a long time that she felt unsure how to respond.

'I'm sorry, I can't even remember your name.'

He smiled. 'It's Greg.'

'Meredith.'

'I know,' he said taking her hand. After he left, Meredith stood for a long time staring at the front door. She ran her fingers across her palm.

John floated up and down the hallway, fuming. The cheek of it - to come into another man's home and come on to his wife, producing some sob story to induce sympathy. It was a wonder he hadn't left a trail of slime behind him.

Of course under normal circumstances Meredith was smart enough to see through such a ploy, but obviously the woman was currently distraught. Anything could happen.

Having returned to the living room, Meredith stood fingering the parcel. She hesitated a second, then feeling for the end of Sellotape with her nails, ripped it across and pulled open the box.

He watched through narrowed slits as she took out one book, then another, pausing to caress the shiny covers, lifting each one to her nose as if it were some exotic flower. She curled up on the sofa, opened one and was soon engrossed.

The minute they had arrived in St Petersburg, Meredith had been captivated by the romance of Russian history - the opulence of the

Tsars, the ideology of the Bolsheviks. Months after the holiday ended, she had borrowed books from the library. He remembered how excited she'd been when she found this course on the Internet, and was ashamed to recall that his reaction had been somewhat dismissive. He had thought it would turn out to be some sort of fad, much like the half-finished embroidery in the sideboard drawer, only ten times as expensive.

But now he wondered whether he had been hasty in his judgement. Might not this be the thing that - well, not helped her get over him, obviously it would take more than a few history books to do that - but at least leave the house, take an interest in life again?

John felt an inner glow. He had had an idea.

Meredith sighed with exasperation. 'Not that dratted magazine again,' she muttered. For the past two weeks it had seemed like the thing was following her around. Each time she thought she had thrown it away, it reappeared again: on the coffee table, across the cooker, once even on the bathroom floor and how it got there she couldn't fathom - reading on the toilet had been John's penchant.

This time, the magazine was lying face-up on top of the kitchen work-surface. 'I am going mad,' she said out loud and wondered, not for the first time, whether this was true. Either that or it was some kind of divine judgement on her recent failure to recycle.

'Right, *this* time you're going into the green box.' A glass wobbled a precarious dance on the shelf above her head before crash landing onto the surface below.

'For heaven's sake!' A few slivers of glass had found their way on top of the magazine and, as Meredith picked it up to slide them into the dustbin, she glanced down at the open pages. 'Hermitage Museum Exhibition Comes to London', the headline announced.

Intrigued, she set the magazine back on the counter and began to read.

Deciding to visit the exhibition and actually doing it were two different things, however. Every day, she pulled on her coat, took a deep breath, opened the front door and stepped onto the doorstep. Yet, on each occasion fate somehow intervened to decree the journey impossible. On Monday, it started to rain - and Meredith could not find an umbrella. On Tuesday, she began to sneeze and suspected she was coming down with a cold. Wednesday had an ominous air to it, while Thursday was tainted by undercurrents of thunder.

On Friday, the sun broke through the clouds and trickled onto the herringbone path in front of the house. Meredith hesitated on the doorstep, thinking about her kitchen cupboards and whether it wouldn't be better to spend the day re-arranging them. Embroiled in indecision, she was oblivious to the door slamming next door, and was, therefore, taken by surprise when a disembodied head appeared from the other side of the hedge, hair stuck up at right angles.

'Hi there,' Greg said.

'Hi.' Meredith stood there, hands knotted together, awkward silence bellowing in her ears.

'Beautiful day, isn't it? After the week we've had I'm not sorry I got this one for my day off.'

'Yes, yes it is. I don't mind crisp, cold days but the rain really gets into you.' The weather - a great British institution. What people in hot countries found to talk about she couldn't imagine.

'So, are you off anywhere exciting?'

'Um, uh yes, there's an exhibition at the V&A.' She produced the half scrunched up page of magazine from her bag and smoothed it out as best she could on top of the hedge.

He peered down at it. 'The one from Russia? I read about that. Fascinating. Of course I remember you said you were interested. There's something emotive about Russian history isn't there? The revolution especially - it captures the imagination I suppose, on both sides. Sorry, I'm rambling.'

'No, I know exactly, what you mean. Sometimes I close my eyes and I feel as though I'm there - actually in the Winter Palace. I can hear the rustling of skirts and the footsteps of the girls as they chase each other through the rooms.' She blushed and looked down at her feet. What an idiot he must think her.

'Yes and later the revolution, whether you agree with communism or not, there is something powerful - beautiful even - about Marxist ideology.'

'And yet the reality is so tainted by corruption.'

'But perhaps no more than capitalism has been?'

Meredith looked up at him, eyes bright. 'Would you like to see the exhibition with me?' She asked and then wished the ground would swallow her whole, sure that he would have a hundred better things to do.

'I'd love to,' he said.

John watched them from the dining room window, a strange sensation in his stomach - or rather in the place his stomach would have been had he had one. All week, he had seen Meredith prepare to go out, had cheered her on, willed her to make it past the doorstep. And each day, he had experienced a growing sense of his own powerlessness at her inability to leave.

On the first day, he had tried to be useful, finding the umbrella and dropping it at - and then on - her feet. After she had kicked it to one side for the third time, he was forced to conclude that rain was not his biggest hurdle.

Then he had tried chivvying her. Banging doors, clattering pots and pans and generally making the house a less than pleasant environment to be in. Meredith had poured herself a large glass of wine, taken a sleeping tablet and pulled the covers over her head - arms wrapped resolutely around the jumper.

Today he had come up with the perfect plan: snooker. She had never stayed in the house for more than five minutes when he had put it on in the past and he saw no reason why today should be any different. It was brilliant, foolproof even, he couldn't think why it hadn't occurred to him before.

But here she was talking to Greg. Not just talking, but actually smiling - laughing a little. Had she forgotten she was supposed to be a grieving widow? Still, she would get rid of him soon, make some excuse and return to the house. Except she didn't. He watched in mystified disbelief as she moved off down the path, stepped onto the pavement and started walking down the road - with *him*.

For the rest of the day, John flittered from room to room like an anxious parent, too unsettled to think of watching the snooker. At 6.05pm she returned, and he couldn't fail to notice her sallow cheeks glowed in a way they hadn't for months. 'It's just the fresh air,' he muttered, but the words sounded hollow and unconvincing, even to him.

The following evening, he hovered over the bed, watching her brush out long, dark coils of hair - had it always been so glossy? - and search for her favourite earrings, which he had hidden under a pillow. She fastened a silver pendent around her neck and smiled into the mirror, turning her head a little to one side as she did so. John felt himself dissolve into waves of mist: he had forgotten how beautiful she was.

Unlocking the chest of drawers, she stood there, one hand resting on top of the jumper. Without thinking, he leant down to kiss her, forgetting this was no longer possible. To his surprise, instead of a cold rush of air he felt warm, solid flesh. She put a hand to her lips.

'John?' He hesitated. If he put his arms around her now, she would feel it, of that he was certain. But was that what he wanted for her? A life of gradual decay, trapped together inside this house, until living and dead became one indistinguishable mass?

A minute passed, then another. She pushed the drawer shut and turned the key, then placed it on top of the dressing table. At the door she paused again. He felt her eyes burn through him - if she saw him now it would all be over.

'Enough,' she said putting a hand to her forehead. 'Enough now.' She stepped out onto the landing, closing the door behind her.

Inside the bedroom time slowed, stopped and ceased to exist.

Greg smoothed over a red and white checked tablecloth and laid out cutlery and glasses. Selecting a bottle of Cabernet Sauvignon from the wooden wine rack in the corner, he eased out the cork and made the bottle the table's centrepiece - an axis from which he hoped the whole night would swing.

'Not too shabby,' he thought, standing back to survey the result. On the wall, a young woman laughed down at him from a mock-ivory frame. He touched her cheek with one fingertip, ran another down her long, fair hair.

'We have company tonight, sweetheart,' he said.

Child's Play

ANAND NAIR

This is an excerpt from **Miles to Go**, *a story set in war-time India. Indu and Savi, seven and nine years old respectively, grow up in a small town, where, theoretically, World War Two is a distant distraction, hardly impinging on their uneventful lives. But Indu's father goes to jail as a freedom fighter and life changes dramatically.*

Thursdays and Sundays were holidays at Indu's school, The Sacred Heart Convent. The state schools closed dutifully on Saturdays and Sundays like the rest of the working world, but the nuns *had* to do something different, if only to establish their superiority. Savi, Indu's best friend, went to a local Primary school, so Sunday was the one day Indu had to spend with Savi.

Some time in the evening on Saturdays, when her *jutka* clip-clopped home from school, Indu would start thinking about playing with Savi. Would Savi's disagreeable father, Chathu, be at home to scream at them? It would be a good Sunday if he was sleeping off a drinking bout from the previous day; he would not emerge from his dark hole of a bedroom till mid-day, and then he would be half-asleep.

Before she set off towards Savi's house in the morning, Indu always checked whether Mathu, Savi's mother, who was the maid at Indu's house, had started sweeping the front yard, making wide semicircles in the dust with her broom. And was

Chathu up and about? She remembered the last time he had seen her playing with Savi.

'Get out,' he had shouted, waving his walking stick. 'Stay the other side of the fence.'

Today, Savi's veranda was empty, so Indu wriggled through the fence at the kitchen end of her house and crossed the narrow path to Savi's mud-brick hut. It still gave her a sense of wrongdoing. When her father was around, going to Savi's house was strictly forbidden. According to him they were 'useless people' and her grandmother called them 'the unwashed tribe next door'.

Now, however, her father was in Vellore Jail, because he was something called a freedom fighter, and Indu could go where she wished.

Indu tiptoed gingerly up the rickety quarry stones, which did duty for steps to Savi's hut; she knew from experience they had a habit of tilting if you caught the edge; she had stubbed her little toe on those a few times. Chathu's dilapidated deck chair was the only furniture on the veranda and his blue-and-white, crumpled *lungi* hung on the back as though he had thrown it there in a hurry. Indu gave the chair a wide berth though Savi's grim father was not sitting on it just then.

When she reached the front door she stopped for a moment and peered into the tiny, cramped corridor, getting her eyes accustomed to the forbidding darkness inside.

'Savi, where are you?' she called uneasily, as she stepped inside. She could smell the mouth-watering, farinaceous smell of roasting cassava, not something made in her own house very often. It was only in the houses of the poor that cassava was used as a staple instead of rice.

'In the kitchen. Come,' Savi shouted out. Indu heard the rustling of dry leaves and knew Savi was in front of the three-stone fireplace shovelling them into it with her hands. In the morning Savi was often to be found there, warming up yesterday's fish curry or straining old rice from the cold water soak that kept it fresh.

Indu forced herself to step into the dark passage leading to Savi; the floor felt gritty and uneven. There was a bedroom on either side and, if you peered in, it was always night in there and smelled of unwashed clothes and damp. Once safe past the rooms, the kitchen was light-filled and airy with a door leading outside, though it hung loose on one hinge. Outside the door was the large half-sphere of the bamboo basket under which Mathu kept her chickens. The dry leaves that Mathu swept up from the compounds where she worked and the coconut fronds she begged off Indu's aunt Devi for firewood were heaped just outside the door. Some were spread on the mud floor in front of the hearth.

Indu found the older girl squatting in front of the fire, on the floor, blowing at the embers through a bamboo pipe. A fine patina of ash had settled on her matted shoulder length hair, which was more brown than black. Indu loved Savi's hair, wavy and thick and long, unlike her own convenient crop.

Savi nudged the roasting cassava out of the fire towards her and beat at it with the bamboo pipe, testing whether the skin had flaked, ready to split open. Satisfied it was done she left it on the floor to cool and turned to Indu who was now squatting beside her.

'Play *kottamkallu*?' she asked. It was Savi who generally took the lead in such important matters as what game to play each day. She was left so much to herself by her mother that she had grown beyond her years. She was also inventive, making up games that could be played with things picked up from their compounds: glistening leaves fallen off the Jack-tree and minuscule, cone-shaped seeds of the *arecanut*.

Mathu did not have much choice except to leave Savi to her own devices. What Chathu gave her for rice and fish each month, after he had drunk most of his salary, did not stretch beyond the middle of the month. She supplemented this income with working in Indu's house, sweeping and swabbing, spreading cow dung on the floors once a week, and beating the life out of clothes on the concrete slab at the back. For this she was given five rupees a month and food for her and Savi. Because of this work she knew her daughter would never go hungry.

'Mmm...' Indu murmured, too eager for the cassava to say anything properly. The two girls started beating at the hot cassava with their palms, loosening the burnt skin from the tuber, then peeling it off to bite greedily into the fluffy white flesh. They opened their mouths and blew *ha-ha* as the hot cassava threatened to burn their tongues. For Savi this would be breakfast but Indu had already eaten her *conjee* of well-cooked rice in its starchy water, and *moong dhal* curry, before she ventured out.

The two girls were so engrossed in their cassava they did not hear the clumsy footsteps outside, the thump of an umbrella on the floor, followed by the shuffle of a weight collapsing on the deck chair. Then someone cleared his throat, hawked and spat noisily.

'Father,' Savi said, standing up quickly, in her haste dropping the remnants of the cassava she was eating. Indu scrambled up too, but before she could escape Chathu was in the kitchen glaring at her, and Savi was nowhere to be seen.

'Where is the other one? Saveee...' he called. His speech was slurred. 'Where is that *nayinde mole, koothicheende mole*?' He stretched out his arm to grab hold of Indu, and then thought better of it. In the process he lost his balance and fell back against the kitchen wall. Indu smelled his sour toddy breath as he glowered at her, and with it the stench of stale sweat.

He heaved himself up slowly and leaned towards Indu. 'Eating my cassava! Mmm...go, go...now - and don't let me see you here again.' The thick blob of mucous, which had hung under his left nostril was now smeared across his cheek.

Indu heard the menace in his voice; no one had ever spoken to her like that. Perhaps he was the reason she was not allowed to go to Savi's house. She ran out of the back door and across the path. Wriggling through the fence she scratched her arm on the wooden post, but didn't stop till she reached her veranda. She was breathless and shaking, glad to be on familiar turf but also certain there would not be any sympathy for her if Devi got to know she had sneaked off next door.

Savi wandered on to Indu's veranda later. 'Kothamkallu?' she asked. In her right hand she loosely held a fistful of stones; they threatened to dribble through her fingers. She sat down carefully on the cement floor, at the edge of the veranda - she would never come further in, as though there were some invisible lines that stopped her. She scattered the stones in her hand in a small spread in front of her. Then she selected her master stone and threw it up to head height in front of her, testing its path. Not satisfied, she repeated the action, scooping up five small stones from off the floor, as the big stone started to descend. She caught her master stone neatly with the same hand and smiled at Indu. Savi was very good at this game.

To Indu, Savi seemed almost a grown-up. Self-sufficient, because she made her own rules, and did not care what the adults thought or did. When she was younger she used to follow Mathu around when she came to work, always a few paces behind, left thumb firmly stuck in mouth. These days the thumb was definitely not in the mouth and Mathu came to work alone.

Indu knew there was no point asking Savi where she had been and why her father was so angry. Savi never said much about what happened in her home, concentrating on the games they played together. It was always Indu who asked questions. When the questions became oppressive, Savi would merely get up and saunter away.

'I thought he was going to hit me,' Indu volunteered, taking care not to *ask* anything this time.

'He won't hit you. Only Amma and me. He's scared of your father.' Indu knew that one angry shout from her father was enough to make her want to pee, but he had never hit her, even that time when she had accidentally pushed one of his law books off the veranda ledge and into the rain. He said he didn't believe in hitting anyone, there were better ways to make children behave.

'But he's not here now.' Indu voice trembled on the *now*; suddenly she wanted her father. Chathu, she was certain, would not have dared shout at her if her father was around.

'That's right. So don't wait for him to save you. We just have to run fast when my father comes back from work. He's always too drunk to chase us.'

For Savi all of this appeared to be totally normal. Indu knew her friend lived in a more precarious and uncertain world, but she had never imagined she needed to run away and hide from her own father. Now Indu had to learn to run as well. And hide?

'Hide where?' Indu asked bemused. There was nowhere to hide in Savi's little house with two rooms and a kitchen.

'In the gully at the back. There is a drumstick tree there and I sit behind it.' Indu had always known there was a narrow path there; it was the place where Chathu's household went to shit since their old stone-and-thatch latrine came down in the last monsoon. Indu wondered what happened when it rained and you had to go. Did you hold an umbrella up with one hand while you did your business? The narrow channel flooded during the rains bringing all the sewage from up the hill. You could see turds and the odd dead, bloated goat floating in that water. Savi in there? Sometimes Savi's world seemed so distant from hers.

'It's filthy,' Indu said. Savi tossed her head, throwing the comment to the winds. It seemed this was not a worry for her. Indu thought about the elaborate cleaning rituals in her own home: rooms swept daily by Mathu, new cow dung spread on the floors every Friday and women in pristine, white clothes, with shining, newly washed hair down their backs, to dry in the mornings.

No, Indu did not want to hide anywhere near that filthy gully; she must find another place for herself.

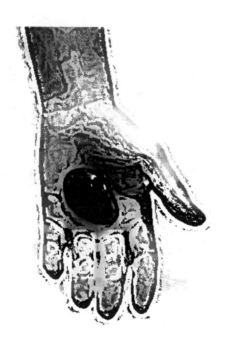

Gestation

HELEN HARDY

I've lived inside your loss,
coiled in the dark
and straining against that skin,
but magically it grows with me,
as now I grow
with her
within.

She stirs, I stir, you stir,
my belly's cauldron
bubbling,
as I reflect upon your role,
and so I see
a mother's arms
can grow on me.

The little words like 'love'
cannot express
the loss, the bonds, the gain,
the knot that's not an agony,
now that it grows,
uncurls
and breathes again.

She lives inside our love,
curled in the warm
and swaddled against that skin,
so magically we grow in me,
as once I grew,
like you,
like her,
within.

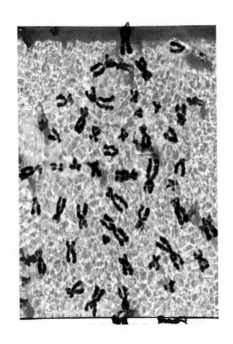

The Gene Pool

DEBI ALPER

This is an excerpt from **The Gene Pool**, *the 5th book in the Nirvana series of thrillers set in South East London. The story so far: When her nephews are involved in a fatal accident, Jen Stern suspects there may be a connection to her sister-in-law's involvement in a campaign to save a local swimming pool threatened with closure. Together with her fellow members of the Nirvana Housing Co-op, she begins to uncover dodgy dealings and local government corruption on a terrifying scale. Jen arranges to meet a contact in Dulwich Woods, in the hope that he can give her some useful information.*

If you've never been to Dulwich and Sydenham Woods you won't know how magical a sensation it is when you first exchange the world of concrete and pollution for the timeless, lush and verdant world of nature. One minute you're haring across the South Circular Road, dodging cars, trucks and buses as they hurtle round the sharp bend trying to beat the red lights; the next you're pushing through a turnstile feeling like Red Riding Hood entering the deepest darkest part of the forest.

Jen approached the tall skinny guy with bleached blonde hair, dressed in jeans and an old duffle coat, who was leaning against the gate. So far, so familiar, she thought, as she shook his hand. Max looked like he could well have been a Nirvanan himself under different circumstances. Together they began the climb up the steep path into the woods. Within a few short yards, the city had been left behind. The dense ancient trees muffled the rumble of traffic, replacing it with birdsong and the rustling of small furry creatures in the thick undergrowth.

'D'you come here often?' Max asked. 'That's a genuine inquiry, by the way, not a chat up line!'

Jen snorted.

'Just as well,' she replied. 'I don't go for cheesy chat ups. Last person who tried that on me ended up on the floor clutching his bollocks!'

To her surprise, she heard Max chuckle.

'So,' he pressed on, unabashed, 'having established I'm not chatting you up, *do* you get up here much?'

Jen grinned. She liked the way he persisted.

'Not really. My kids are a bit too feral to be released into the wild. I've got twins,' she explained. 'We came up here a couple of times in the summer with a picnic but you can't get a double buggy up the paths.'

They'd reached the top of the tarmac track. Behind the trees and fence on their right stretched the open expanse of the golf club. In front of them, a narrow muddy path meandered deeper into the woods. To their left was a red brick footbridge over a steep-sided valley, choked with brambles and dead ferns.

They stood at the centre of the bridge and looked down through the trees.

'It used to be a railway line,' Max said. 'Hard to believe now. You heard of Pissarro? He was an impressionist artist. There's quite a famous painting he did of the view from this bridge when the trains were still running.'

'There used to be trains here?'

'Oh, yeah. It was built to serve the original Crystal Palace in the mid nineteenth century. They demolished the track in the 1950s.'

Max pointed along the valley, which Jen could now imagine echoing with the sounds of steam trains carrying middle-class Victorians to the massive glass exhibition centre a few miles away to the south.

'There's an old tunnel at the top end,' Max said. 'Shall we head that way?'

As they trudged up the footpath deeper into the woods, Jen wondered how to broach the subject of the swimming pools. After a while, she became aware that Max was talking, presumably unaware that she hadn't heard a word he was saying. Jen gave herself a shake. Some kind of crap investigator she was. Everyone says the most important skill is listening. And not just to what's going on in your own head either.

It turned out that what she had missed so far was an exposition of the natural delights the woods had to offer. Max was an unexpected mine of information, but once she had established the information being offered was not what she had come to hear, her focus began to waver again. Lists of wild flowers washed over her. Descriptions of the three different types of woodpeckers breeding there, as well as tawny owls and sparrow hawks ... Nationally endangered bees, wasps and butterflies ... One hundred and seventy four species of fungi...

'Stop!' Jen said, digging her heels in and grabbing Max's jacket sleeve. 'Stop right there!'

'What? Have you seen something? There are some sculptures carved into the living wood just over there...'

'No,' Jen said shaking her head. 'It's not the sculptures. Nor the nuthatches or the wild garlic or the green fucking woodpecker or the hairy bloody woodrush.'

She looked at the hurt expression on Max's face and sighed with exasperation.

'Look, I'm sorry,' she said. 'This is all really interesting and in another life I'd want to spend time hearing this stuff. And I'm impressed, really I am. It's just that my time's limited...'

Max shrugged. Jen could see he was trying not to look disappointed.

'No, I'm sorry,' he muttered, scuffing his toe into a patch of leaf mould. 'I get a bit carried away sometimes.'

He sighed and tilted his head to stare up at the canopy of leaves twisting above them in the breeze. It was a cold crisp day and the sky was clear. A distant aeroplane trail wafted and curled in the upper atmosphere.

'It's just that life out there can be so shit at times.' He made a sweeping gesture to indicate the world beyond the trees. 'I come here to escape. I'm one of a group of volunteers who clear paths and fix fences and stuff. It's a way for me to keep my head straight and not go round kicking fat cat bureaucrats.'

Jen laughed.

'Personally, I thinking kicking fat cats is just as healthy a way to get rid of your frustrations, but I take your point.'

'And I take yours,' Max said, with a rueful smile. 'There's a bench up there by the lake. Let's sit there and talk about what you came here for.'

The bench was carved from an ancient tree trunk and wasn't that comfortable. It was placed near a small reed-clogged pond in the middle of the valley where the train tracks would have run fifty years earlier. The trees were less dense here and there was a feeling of openness not present in the deep woods. Jen hoped it would bode well for Max opening up too.

The first good sign was when Max pulled a flask of coffee from his rucksack.

'Want some?' he asked. 'It's black I'm afraid …'

He filled a plastic beaker with the murky-looking liquid and handed it to her.

'So, what do you want to know?' he said, leaning back on the bench and narrowing his eyes against the sharp winter light.

Jen took a sip of the coffee. Not as strong as she would choose, but welcome nevertheless. She put the beaker on the bench next to her and, pulling out Rizlas and tobacco, rolled a cigarette. Max refused her offer of a smoke with a distracted shake of his head.

'Can we start with Splashland?' Jen asked, lighting the fag. 'Sue said you worked there before you went to Wood Mount.'

'Huh!' Max shuddered. 'I'm beginning to feel like I'm cursed or something. I go to work at a place and a few months later it closes!

I've started to wonder if I should be taking it personally. There have I been, ranting on for months about inefficiency and bureaucratic wankers and corruption, and I suddenly thought this morning - what if it's me? What if I have some savage kind of karma that follows me around, mixes with chlorine and becomes combustible?'

He stared into the distance looking gloomy.

'Splashland?' Jen prompted.

She was beginning to feel she was wasting her time. Max seemed like a nice enough guy but it looked like he had no real solid information. It was lovely to have a walk in the woods, but as far as helping her investigation of the pools was concerned...

So it came as a surprise when Max began to speak. The words spilled out, the only impediment being that he was talking with his jaw clenched.

'Splashland was a disaster even before it opened,' he said. 'They always make a huge deal out of consulting with the community and then blame everyone else when all the stupid errors come to light later. And I mean *really* stupid things. Like no poolside space for parents to watch their kids swim. No toilet in the nappy changing space - which incidentally you can't even get a single buggy into, let alone one of those double ones you have. Basic common sense stuff. You can't blame the public for not having specified they wanted those things. People are entitled to assume that if vast quantities of public money are being spent, there's going to be some stuff that you can leave up to the so-called experts to ensure they get right.'

Max poked his toe at a leaf and bent to pick up a tiny golden beetle.

'Look at that,' he mused. 'This is the only known location in London for this little guy. He's ...'

'Max!'

'Sorry.' Max placed the beetle back on the ground and covered it over with the dead leaf. 'So, where was I? Yeah, Splashland. So it opens with this huge fanfare and everyone's really impressed cos it looks so modern and clean and everything and it's a great new resource for the local community etc, etc. And some people are muttering about all the stupid stuff like not being able to watch their kids' swimming lessons, but otherwise everyone's pretty happy. There's teething problems of course, but we're told that always happens with a brand new facility. Problems with the boiler, the pump - that kind of thing. Then there was the big problem you probably heard about with the chemical leak?'

Jen finished her coffee and handed back the beaker.

'Is it OK to drop this here?' she asked, holding out her fag butt. 'I don't know about the leak. My brain's been pretty mushy these last couple of years - I'm sure I've missed quite a bit. Assume I know nothing, OK?'

Max took the butt and put it in his pocket.

'It's bio-degradable,' he explained. 'But it still doesn't belong here. We try not to leave anything behind or take anything away... Right, the leak. So this one day, it's during the Easter holidays and the pool's packed. I'm on duty and you know how sometimes something can sneak up on you? You only vaguely start to notice all's not well at first and then suddenly - wham! It's major panic time! It's not like an accident or someone nearly drowning. That kind of thing you zap straight into crisis mode, but this just sort of gradually dawned on me.'

He tailed off and cocked his head to one side.

'Hear that?' he said. 'That's a nuthatch.'

'Max!' Jen yelled so loud that Max, his ears straining to hear the faint birdsong, jumped as though she had hit him.

'Shit!' he said. 'Not so loud! You'll disturb the wild life.'

'Max, please. I'm going wild here myself. I haven't got long...'

'Sure. Sorry... again,' Max muttered with evident reluctance. 'So I started to notice a lot of the kids seemed to have streaming eyes. There were some really young kids in the pool and a couple of them started crying like they were in pain. One of the mums came up to me and said the chlorine seemed really strong and as soon as she said it I noticed the smell was all wrong. Then this kid started struggling for breath in the deep end. I thought he was having an asthma attack. I jump in and get him out and then Dougie - he's the other lifeguard on duty - says to me he thinks we've got a problem.

So we do a test and the chlorine balance is way out. Big time danger level. By this time we've got people staggering out of the pool coughing and spluttering and my eyes were really burning and my throat was raw, like I'd just eaten a glass sandwich.'

'So what happened?'

'What happened was that we had to evacuate the building. All these people huddled outside in their bathing costumes and no coats or anything. Little kids, mums with babies... Fleets of bloody ambulances. The chemical balance was supposed to be calibrated automatically. But when they had an inquiry afterwards they said it had been tampered with. "Human error," they said. Having spent squillions on an automatic system, guess who gets blamed if something goes wrong?'

'Did they discipline anyone?'

'No, of course not. They couldn't prove a thing. Questioned everyone on duty over and over, said they'd sorted it and reopened the pool again a few days later.'

Jen frowned.

'But that means - if they never uncovered the real cause...'

'Exactly. Same thing could happen again. I mean anyone can make mistakes but I always thought the point was you're supposed to learn from them. Anyway, they sacked Dougie a week later for eating a burger on poolside and some people were saying he must have had something to do with the chemical business after all.'

'But you don't think so?'

'Nah. Dougie was a bit of a prat, but I can't imagine him doing something like that. I mean, what for? Why would he bother?'

'D'you know where he is now?'

'Yeah. Back home in Sydney where he only has to worry about getting skin cancer.'

Jen checked the time on her mobile and confirmed she didn't have much of it left.

'Can you tell me about Splashland closing?'

Max peered at her through narrowed eyes.

'Why is it I sometimes think you sound really official?' he asked. 'This feels like I'm being interviewed...'

Jen knew you get nothing for nothing. If she wanted Max to continue, she would have to give him something in return.

'Look,' she said. 'I'm really suspicious about all this, but there are personal reasons for my interest. I don't want to go into too much detail at this point, but certain people I know were recently involved in what might or might not have been an accident. The line I'm following is whether any of the people involved in this pool business are corrupt rather than incompetent. And whether that corruption could lead to actual violence.'

Max looked at her in surprise and gave a low whistle.

'Violence? What - like beating people up you mean?'

'That and worse. I need to get a sense if that's something they'd be capable of.'

'Well, I guess that depends on who 'they' are, doesn't it? Are you talking about the council? Or Directions? I guess you know they operate the leisure services in the borough ... Then there's the consultants, the construction company, all those other subsidiaries ... They're all out to line their own pockets. That's the problem when you get private companies vying for public money. It doesn't work. Their priorities are too different. All they care about is their profit margin. But operating public facilities shouldn't be about that. It should be about giving local people the best possible service. I mean, when the floor collapsed at Splashland - just a few weeks after the chemical business - do you blame the construction company? They're quite capable of cutting corners to save themselves a bob or two. But then you could say the same for Directions and the council...'

'But if it was a problem caused by cost-cutting that would be out in the open, wouldn't it? People would know about it. I mean, it's crass and stupid and backward thinking, but it wouldn't be actual corruption...'

'Not unless the money they saved made their way into someone's pocket...'

Jen nodded. They were getting somewhere at last.

'Do you have anyone in mind?'

If Jen thought she was nearing her goal, she was destined for disappointment.

'No idea,' Max replied with an apologetic shrug. 'We never see anyone apart from the lot in charge at the pool, who are right at the bottom of the management food chain, and the occasional biggish wig from Directions or Leisure and Rec at the council.'

Pulling her coat tighter round her, Jen shivered and stood up. Sitting down for so long had allowed the chill to enter her bones and it was close to the time she'd need to leave anyway. The shadows were lengthening as the sun dipped below the level of the trees, taking the last of its feeble warmth with it. Max also stood and together they made their way back down the centre of the valley.

'I will tell you this though,' Max said as they walked. 'Some of these people are ambitious and some of them are ruthless and some of them will stop at nothing if it ends up with them making serious money. I can't give you any specific info about individuals but nothing would surprise me. I mean, take the business with Wood Mount. I could've predicted how it would go. They run it down; they have a warped and phoney irrelevant consultation, which they can then safely ignore by saying it's a health and safety issue and the pools are too dangerous after all. I can't prove anything but my instincts tell me someone somewhere is going to making some serious quids over this. As far as I'm concerned, this stinks worse than that chlorine leakage. You find who stands to make the money and you'll find the person who'd have most to gain. Or lose. If anyone's going to be resorting to violence, that'll be your man.'

They had reached the entrance to the wood. Behind them the branches waved and creaked, the birds chattered and the woodland creatures snuffled. Ahead of them the traffic roared, exhausts pumped and drivers fumed.

Max turned to Jen.

'Sorry,' he grimaced. 'Haven't been much help, have I?'

'No, you have,' she reassured. 'It's been really interesting. I never expected you to say, oh yes, Mr X is your man and this is where you can reach him. And here's a photo of him committing acts of extreme violence by the way.'

Max grinned.

'You take care, Jen,' he said. 'If you *are* right and someone involved in this shit is capable of resorting to violence to protect their interests…'

'I know,' Jen interjected. 'Don't worry. I can take care of myself.'

She said goodbye and turned to leave, looking for a gap in the traffic but Max called her back.

'If it was me,' he said, 'the first place I'd look is the council itself. Whoever's in charge of allocating the contracts is going to have a lot of power and they'd be the link between everyone else.' He shrugged. 'Sorry - not much help, but it's just a thought, y'know?'

Jen smiled at him.

'It's a good thought,' she said. 'Cheers, Max.'

As she ran across the busy road she reflected the afternoon had not been a complete waste of time after all. She had heard some interesting information about the way the leisure facilities operated in the borough as well as having a possible starting point for her investigation, which was more than she'd had before.

She'd also found out a lot more about the elusive purple hairstreak butterfly. Her priority lay with the swimming pools, whereas Max's… Safe on the pavement, Jen looked back. Max was still standing by the gate, gazing up the track into the woods.

'Hey, Max!' she yelled, trying to be heard above the thunder of the traffic. He turned and she cupped her hands to her mouth to channel her voice.

'You should give up that job, you know. Get one as a park ranger or tree looker-afterer or something.'

He laughed and waved his hand in acknowledgement. Before Jen had time to walk more than half a dozen paces, he was already making his way back into the woods.

A Sideways Step

RACHAEL DUNLOP

Henry felt his father's hand on his shoulder. 'C'mon son, time to go.'

Henry stifled a sigh and put the binoculars on the window ledge.

'Where are we going today, Dad?'

'I thought we could go see a film and...' Henry's dad let the sentence trail off: somewhere in the depths of his pocket, his Blackberry had started to ring with its familiar cheery chirrup. He backed out of the room, his phone plugged to his ear.

Henry turned back to the window and picked up his binoculars. He had been spying on the playground from his bedroom for an hour now but so far he had seen nothing out of the ordinary. Henry was sure it was just a matter of time, though. He just needed to keep watching. He hoped his dad's grand Saturday plans would be sidelined by some emergency at work. Henry didn't like it when his dad tried so hard. It made him squirm under the expectation that he should be having a good time. Before the divorce, doing stuff with Dad just happened. Now it was an event.

Henry focused his attention on the playground. It was September, and the sprinklers had been turned off for a few weeks now. Through his binoculars, Henry could see the grey-brown sediment the water had left in the scooped-out tarmac around the drains. The paddling pool had been drained too: there were early-falling leaves collecting in the corners, along with plastic cup-lids skewered with straws, and mottled scraps of paper, bleached of ink. It was as if the world was sloughing off its warm summer skin, revealing something cooler, paler and harder beneath.

Henry swept the binoculars around the playground in a slow arc. Nothing. He let his gaze settle, unfocused, on the swings, and then he saw what he'd been looking for. A vertical slash in the air, four feet long and hovering just above the ground, gold against the autumn grey of the sunless afternoon. He lowered his binoculars and it was gone. Henry knew: it was his turn.

Henry's dad had picked this flat because it had a playground next door. 'We'll be able to kick a ball around, you can ride your bike,' he said on Henry's first weekend visit. Henry had dropped his overnight bag on the bed and looked out the bedroom window. He smiled. It looked like a nice playground. That had been six months ago, and neither Henry nor his dad had ever set foot in that playground.

When the first kid had disappeared, one Saturday morning back in June, there was a huge hullaballoo and the playground closed for a week. The girl had been playing by the climbing frames, then disappeared. Actually disappeared, right in front of her friends.

'She sort of stepped sideways and was gone,' one pinch-faced eight-year-old had told the gathered reporters. Henry watched the report on the local news and hoped the playground would re-open soon.

A few weeks later, one Sunday afternoon, it happened again. A mother stopped to knock sand out of her toddler's shoes, turned, and found her older son had vanished. This time, the playground wasn't closed down. The police came and went, life carried on.

Soon children were going missing almost every weekend, but no one seemed to notice. In fact, the more children disappeared, the less anyone seemed to notice - except for Henry. He watched the playground from his bedroom window, when he wasn't being taken to the zoo, to a football match, to the museum. Henry never saw it happen, but he could see *when* it happened. For a fraction of a moment, everything in the playground would pause. Balls were dropped, skipping ropes sagged, bikes wobbled as their riders neglected to pedal. Stillness rippled in a small swift wave through the playground, then all was normal again. All except for a parent gazing around with a puzzled look, like they'd just walked into a room but forgotten what they came for. Like they had lost something they had never had. Henry knew what he had lost, and now he thought he knew where to find it. He just had to wait for his turn.

'Good news, Henry, we can go to the cinema after all ... Henry?'

Henry didn't turn around, but kept his binoculars fixed on that long streak of otherness hanging in the air. 'I don't want to go to the cinema today, Dad. I want to go to the playground.'

'The...?'

'The playground. Out there.'

Henry's dad looked out the window, with a confused expression on his face. It was as if he'd never seen the place before. 'I don't think so, Henry. A film. Let's go see a film.'

But Henry was gone, unhearing, heading out the door. He lolloped down the stairs and was soon outside and in the playground. He put his hands to his neck and realised he had left his binoculars behind. He'd have to find it some other way. It was his turn.

Henry circled the swings, his hands stretched out in front of him. Nothing. From the gate, his dad called him: 'Henry. Come back,' but already it seemed like his heart wasn't in it. Henry turned from the sound of his father's voice. There it was: a fold in the air, like the place where a pair of curtains meets. Henry took a sideways step and disappeared.

Henry stepped into golden warmth. His eyes were dazzled by low rays of autumn sunshine, split by the swaying chains of the swings. Henry heard his name being called - his parents were sitting on a bench on the far side of the playground. His father waved then dropped an arm around Henry's mother's shoulder. They were smiling.

Through the closing gap in the air, Henry could see his other father, as grey as the dusty tarmac under his feet. He was shaking his head, casting unseeing eyes around the playground, turning to leave. The gap closed and Henry felt a brief pinch of sadness then wondered what it was he had been staring at. He couldn't remember.

He sat down on a swing and started pushing himself backwards and forwards. This was a nice playground, he thought.

'Mum, Dad, look at me!' he called as he dug the scuffed toes of his trainers into the ground and propelled himself into the sky.

The Festival Finale

DANIEL MAITLAND

Maria was lost
at the Festival Finale.
Fireworks exploded above her
and horns and whistles deafened her ears.
She had looked for Richard everywhere
and was pathetically close to tears.

What hopes she'd had:
for this day.
And for Richard.
Who would have been very easy to find
- had she looked,
crotch deep in the girl with feather headdress
from the Calypso float.

Optimum Weight

RICHARD WOODHOUSE

Everyone in Weeton liked Joe Grande. As he huffed and puffed his way along Narrow Street the shopkeepers and passers-by all had kind words for him. How was Mrs Grande today? What a dapper suit he was wearing. How was his visit to the big city? And all agreed his pies were absolutely the best for miles. He smiled and asked about their lives and loved ones in return.

But by the time he reached the premises of Dr Pipette, Joe's smile had disappeared because he was struggling for breath and turning a worrying shade of red. The receptionist held out a glass of water.

'Thank you.'

'Sit yourself down, Mr Grande,' she said, 'The doctor will be with you soon.'

Joe examined the waiting room chairs. They seemed rather small and fragile, so he stood and supped the water.

'The doctor will see you now.'

With a furrowed brow he stepped inside.

'Ah, Joe, Joe, Joe, a pleasure as always.' Dr Pipette leapt out of his chair and gave him a hearty handshake. 'I've not forgotten how much you made from me at cards last week.' He winked and Joe's whole body chuckled.

'Lady Luck, Paul, Lady Luck.'

'Lady Luck be damned.' The physician sat. 'Now, what can I do for you?'

'I believe you summoned me.'

'I did?' He rummaged through his notes. 'Ah, yes, indeed.' He scowled at some medical results and shook his head. 'Everything is up, Joe, everything: cholesterol, blood pressure, blood glucose.' He gave Joe a steely look. 'You are greatly increasing your chances of diabetes, heart failure and cancer.'

Joe looked abashed.

The doctor stood. 'Hop onto the scales.'

'Do I have to?'

'Yes.'

Joe dragged himself across the room.

'How tall are you, Joe?'

'Five foot nine and half.'

'Five foot nine,' the doctor repeated, looking at a chart by the scales.

'And a half.'

'The optimum weight for someone of your height is 12 stone and 2 pounds. And you are?'

'Are you trying to humiliate me?'

'No, Joe, I'm trying to communicate that this is serious - deadly serious.'

Joe stepped onto the scales. The arrow flew like a rocket and shuddered to a halt. The pair peered at the weight. Dr Pipette coughed and turned away.

'I know, I know.' Joe sighed heavily.

'It's all about will power. Talk it through with Anne. Devise a plan.'

As Joe stepped off the scales he saw himself in the surgery mirror. Most of his body extended beyond its rectangle. His friend put an arm about his shoulders. 'Just imagine what a slim Joe Grande could do.'

Joe imagined his oval shape deflating into one that fitted the mirror.

'I'd leave Weeton'

'Leave, why?

'It's too small.'

The doctor looked sceptical. 'Better a big fish…'

Joe shook his head. 'The bakery could really grow in the city.'

'It's quite a risk.'

'That's for sure...'

When Joe tramped back into the shop his wife, Anne, could sense something was wrong.

'Cup of coffee, dear?'

'If you want.'

He walked between the displays of breads, cakes and pies.

'How about an almond croissant?'

'Okay. Uh, no, better not.'

Joe disappeared into the rear of the shop. Anne discovered him upstairs sitting on his bed gripping the duvet and staring out the window. She put the coffee on the bedside table and sat next to him.

'Whatever's wrong, Joe?'

'I'm too fat.'

She cuddled him. 'You wouldn't be you if you were skinny.'

'I barely made it back from the doctor's just now.' He looked at her. 'I don't want to be like this for the rest of my life. I've got plans, big plans.'

'Did the doctor tell you to lose weight again?'

'Yes. But I've no will power. I'll just eat myself into the grave, I know I will.'

'Now stop that kind of talk right away. You'll find a way.'

That evening when Joe was searching the Internet for advice on losing weight, an advert caught his eye. It announced a new product - TITANUM CONDENSIDE - that was guaranteed to reduce your weight fast. The proclamation of a guarantee made a usually sceptical Joe click the link. Up came a flashy website promoting tiny pink pills that were "the biggest thing since Viagra," and, "guaranteed to get you to your optimum weight." Joe nodded thoughtfully. Then the site explained the pills had been developed by NASA. That was the clincher. If it was good enough for NASA, it was good enough for him. Joe made an order.

Two days later Joe was putting the final touches to a new collection of miniature gateaux he was developing (six exquisite mouth watering morsels of loveliness ranging from oozy cream extravagance to dark chocolate decadence), when he became aware of someone behind him. It was Arnold, the postman. Joe turned and presented his creations to him with a flourish.

'Magnificent, aren't they?'

'Bit on the small side, I reckon.'

Joe raised a forefinger. 'Ah, but big on flavour, Arnold. Would you like to try one?'

'No, I'll stick to my beef pasty thanks.'

With a sigh Joe got the pasty.

Arnold rummaged in his sack. 'I've got something for you.'

Joe passed the pasty. Arnold passed a padded envelope. They said goodbye and Joe waddled quickly to the back of the shop.

Inside the envelope was a silver foil package with TITANUM CONDENSIDE written in flourescent green letters. Joe ripped it open. Shook out the silver sheets of pills and grabbed the instructions. After a quick skim, he got himself a glass of water, popped out a tiny pink pill and swallowed it. For a moment he stood there half expecting to shrink like Alice, but nothing odd occurred. Chuckling at himself he went back to his baking and his big dreams.

As the weeks passed, Anne was pleased to see her husband become increasingly positive.

'I'm losing weight,' Joe announced one day, patting his firkin tummy.

'Oh, Joe, well done.' She kissed him on both cheeks. 'How much have you lost?'

He walked over to the scales in the corner of their bedroom.

'Just over one and a half stone.' He beamed.

'Bless me. That's amazing. I had been worried because you didn't seem to be eating less.'

He coughed. 'Ah, well, I've been cutting out snacks.'

Joe continued to take the pills secretly and Anne continued to be impressed. After two further weeks the time came to revisit Dr Pipette.

'How's the diet been going? I've seen your mini gateaux - must be a great temptation.'

'Have you tried one, Paul?'

'A little too rich for me.'

Joe shook his head. 'No one buys them. This village is incapable of appreciating fine food.'

'Weeton doesn't like change. Now, on the scales please.' The doctor peered down. 'My word, you've lost four stone!'

Joe bowed in satisfaction.

'You wouldn't guess to look at you,' said the doctor.

'It's the suit, I need a smaller suit,' Joe said dismounting.

'If you keep this up you will reach your optimum weight in no time.'

'I'll be so skinny, you won't recognise me,' Joe joked.

The doctor tapped his head with a finger. 'I said it was only a matter of will power.'

Two months later, Anne came home one evening with a gift for Joe - four pairs of patterned pants.

'They're rather loud,' he said.

'They're the biggest M&S do, but they are the smallest I've bought you in a long while and no mistake.'

He held the pair up to the bedroom window. The sun filtered through the pattern of bananas. 'Not too sure I can get into them right now, but thank you, my dear, it's a kind thought.'

'How much have you lost now?'

'Almost eight stone.' He pecked her on the forehead.

'Eight stone? You must be able to get into these.'

'Don't think so,' Joe said.

'Come on, get those trousers off.'

'I was going downstairs to watch Great British Menu.'

'It will only take a moment.' She grabbed hold of his trouser button and undid it.

'Restrain yourself, woman.'

His trousers fell about his feet as if they were revealing a bronze sculpture. Instead they revealed Joe's pale legs and belly. Anne tugged the trousers over his slippers.

'Close the curtains at least?' Joe protested.

'Who's going to see, silly? Now pants off.'

'No. Anyone could look up. I have my reputation to think of.'

'Let's see just how large your reputation is.' She clawed him down his chest and began to pull at his pants.

'I can see resistance is futile.'

Joe stepped out of his slippers, took off the pants, circled them in the air and tossed them onto the bed.

'Try these on, they're made of extra sexy silk,' she said with a kiss.

He felt the pants, nodded with approval and stepped into them. They past his knees okay, and his thighs, but when they struck bottom the pants became stuck.'

'I don't understand it,' Anne said tugging at them. 'Are you sure you've lost eight stone?'

'Of course I am.' The pants fell around his feet.

'Well you don't look any smaller to me.'

'Are you talking about my tummy, or my rolling pin?' he said with a smirk.

She looked down. 'Hmmm, I think I better close those curtains after all, big boy.'

Later, when Joe was undressing for bed, his wife's comments returned to him. He examined himself in the mirror and had to admit he did not look much slimmer. The dreadful thought occurred to him that something was wrong with the scales. He looked around for something to weigh. On his bedside cabinet were three fat cookbooks. Placing one after another on the scales he established to his own satisfaction that the scales were indeed working. Consoled, he felt it would only be a matter of time before he reached his optimum weight.

Despite this, he now began to take two of the pink slimming pills a day. And sure enough his weight continued to tumble. Unfortunately, his girth remained the same. One morning it all became too much. In a fit of rage he picked up the scales and threw them out of the window, determined never to look at them again.

His resolve only lasted a week. It was a hot afternoon, Anne was out shopping and Joe had just taken a shower. Wrapped in a towel he went to his stash of slimming pills. There was only one pill left. He swallowed it and looked at the packet. Guaranteed to reduce your weight, it said. Guaranteed to get you to your optimum weight, it promised. Joe crushed the packet and threw it back in his bedside drawer. He wouldn't be wasting any more money on them!

He looked at himself in the wardrobe mirror. He looked the same size he had always been. Joe simply couldn't understand it. It made no sense. His heart sank. He had been conned. At least no-one knew about his foolishness. With a peculiar mix of anger and curiosity he found himself compelled to know what his weight was right now. He flew down the stairs into the back garden, and found the scales hidden in a pile of crushed chrysanthemums. Joe placed them on the patio and centred the needle. Furtively he discarded his towel and stepped on board.

The needle did not move. Joe peered closer. It remained at zero. That couldn't be right. He got off and then on again. Perhaps he had broken them? In frustration he jumped up and… I would like to say down, but he did not come down. He continued to rise into the air. Up and up Joe went. He flailed and tried to grab a nearby magnolia, but a slight gust of wind wafted him away.

'Help!' he cried.

Joe clamped his hands over his mouth as the full horror of the situation hit him. He was floating over the roof of his house completely butt naked. Placing his hands over his crotch he prayed no one would notice him. He didn't care if he floated to Peru as long as no one saw him. Unfortunately, no sooner had he begun to float above Narrow Street than a young lad happened to notice a shadow moving on the ground and looked up.

'Hey, Mum, it's the baker.' He pointed and his mother looked up. Her eyes widened.

'Turn away Bobby, turn away.'

The boy shouted, 'The baker's in the air, the baker's all bare.'

Joe knew the game was up. One by one everyone in Weeton came out to look up at the peculiar pink cloud that was the naked Joe Grande. Arnold, the postman, waved. The vicar crossed himself. The children laughed and his wife fainted. The only member of the community with any wits was Dr Pipette.

'We have to get him down,' he cried.

'Pop him with a gun,' Bobby shouted.

'Throw him a rope,' suggested Arnold.

Joe's face was puce with embarrassment. Why, oh why, did I take those pills?

'He's lost too much weight somehow,' said the doctor. 'We need to make him heavier.'

'Throw him some doughnuts,' guffawed Bobby.

'Be quiet,' scolded his mother.

The doctor watched Joe float over the parish church and scratched his head when two passing magpies decided to alight on his friend. The villagers' sniggers turned to whooping when they realised the weight of the birds was making Joe descend to within inches of the church's weather vane.

'Grab it, Joe!' they yelled. 'Grab it.'

The thought of exposing his rolling pin and dough balls made Joe hesitate. It looked too late when, finally, he did reach out, but somehow he still managed to grab the weathercock, first with one hand then with the other.

The crowd cheered.

Only when Dr Pipette arrived at the top of the church tower did he dare contemplate letting go.

'I've got you,' said his friend.

The old vicar clambered up, his lungs rattling for air. In his hands was a Union Jack.

'Flag' he gasped, pointing at Joe.

Joe and the doctor looked at each other.

'M - Modesty,' the vicar blurted, throwing Joe the flag.

The pair finally understood. Joe wrapped himself in the Union Jack.

'Come on, let's take you home,' said Dr Pipette.

'No, no. Not till they've all gone.'

The doctor and vicar peered down at the crowd below. 'All right.' They led him down inside the church where a dazed Anne was waiting.

'Oh Joe, what have you done?' she said with sympathy and dread.

By the time the crowd had dispersed stars were twinkling in a black sky. Joe and Anne hurried back home. As soon as he had shut the front door, Joe ran upstairs, threw off the Union Jack, and got into bed.

'We need to talk,' Anne said, walking in.

Cocooned in the comfort of his duvet Joe moaned, 'Go away.'

'How did you lose so much weight and still stay the same size? It's not natural.'

'Leave me alone.'

She sat beside him. 'I'm staying right here until you tell me the truth, Joe Grande.'

An uncomfortable silence followed. Eventually Joe's arm snaked from beneath the cover and pulled open his bedside drawer. After rummaging inside, he threw a crumpled silver package onto the bed. Anne picked it up and flattened it out.

'Oh Joe. What have you done?'

'"They were guaranteed,' he said.

'Did you read the small print?'

'They were invented by NASA.'

'NASA?' Anne examined the leaflet then shook her head. 'That stands for Natural Alternative Slimming Aids, you numpty.'

A wary eye peered from beneath the cover. 'What?'

'You've been conned, love.'

He groaned and disappeared beneath the duvet.'

'Optimum Weight indeed,' she scoffed throwing the box into the bin.

From that moment on, Joe refused to get out of bed. His appetite for food and life evaporated. Anne told him he was acting childishly and believed he would eventually snap out of it. He didn't. Days went by and weeks went by and still Joe remained under the duvet. Anne became increasingly worried for his health. She enticed him with roasted meats and fine cheeses. She tempted him with fresh shellfish and devilish desserts. Joe just looked at it all and told her take it away.

'This has got to stop,' she said finally.

'Leave me alone.'

'What about your plans to open a little shop in the big city? You said the mini gateaux would be huge there.'

'It doesn't matter anymore. I'm just a big fat embarrassment. One enormous joke. I don't know why you stay with me.'

A tear formed in Anne's eye as she left the room.

The weeks of confinement turned into months. Anne contacted Dr Pipette. He came to the house and she told him all about the pink pills. 'He won't eat or leave his bed,' she said. 'I've never seen him like this before.'

'You are looking peaky yourself, Anne, if I may say so.'

She pulled at her curly hair. 'I'm going out my mind with worry. I can't sleep. The shop's…'

Anne burst into tears. The doctor held her hand and smiled. She tried to reciprocate, but her mouth only quivered.

'Let me have a word with him,' he said.

The doctor found Joe hiding in his bed. 'My dear Joe, this will not do. You have to get out of bed and get on with your life.'

'You all laughed at me,' said a pathetic voice.

The doctor sat on the bed. 'You've lived here all your life. We are your friends.'

'I should have left years ago. Weeton will be the death of me.'

'For heaven's sake, come out from under that duvet.'

Joe emerged like a frightened turtle.

'You've lost weight,' the doctor noted.

'That's impossible, I weighed nothing before.'

'You look thinner, I mean.'

'Good. Perhaps I'll disappear all together.'

Joe shrank back into his duvet shell.

The doctor stroked his chin for a moment then went downstairs. He told a bemused Anne he would return in six weeks. She had hoped for some change after the doctor's visit, but Joe remained immovable. By turns she chastised and cajoled him, ignored and lavished attention on him - all to no avail. At the end of the sixth week she was emotionally spent. When Dr Pipette arrived at the door she looked at him blankly.

'Yes?'

'I've come to see Joe.'

'Oh, him.'

She trudged to the kitchen, leaving the doctor to go upstairs. Despite the early hour, the bedroom curtains were closed. The atmosphere was dim and oppressive. On the bedside cabinet lay a curled sandwich and a glass of water.

'Joe, it's me, Dr - I mean Paul.'

'Paul?'

The doctor perched on the bed. 'Paul Pipette.'

'Where am I?'

The doctor pulled the duvet down and gazed at Joe. The jolly mound of a man had been replaced by a shrunken, waxy figure with a bushy beard.

'You're at home in bed, my friend,' said the doctor.

'Is this a dream?'

'No, this is real, and time for you to get up.'

'Get up?' Joe's dark eyes looked baffled.

'Yes. I need to know if you can.'

'I don't care if I can.'

The doctor took the glass of water and placed it in Joe's hand. 'Drink this.' Joe parted his dry lips and drank. 'Now come, I want you to stand.'

With gentleness and firmness the doctor encouraged his confused friend to slide out of bed and stand.

'Let's see if you can walk, eh?' Joe shuffled around the bed with him. 'Now stand there.'

'No, don't let go of me.' Joe held his friend's hand tight.

'I'll only be a moment.'

Pulling his hand from Joe's sweaty grip, the doctor went over to the curtains and snapped them open. Sunlight blazed about the room. Joe let out a cry and closed his eyes.

'Open your eyes, Joe,' the doctor said. 'Open your eyes.'

Joe's eyelids parted. As his eyes adjusted to the glare he saw a naked man appear before him, a slim naked man with a beard. Suddenly frightened he said, 'Who's that? Who else is here, Paul?'

'No one, it's you, Joe. It's you.'

Joe raised his hands to his face and pinched it. He pulled his fingers through the beard and patted the body until he could no longer deny he was indeed looking at himself in the wardrobe mirror.

'I'm thin!' He turned and pressed his friend's face between his hands. 'I-am-thin!'

The doctor smiled a squashed smile. 'Yes, you are.'

They both laughed. Joe attempted a jig but became dizzy and had to sit.

'Now you take it easy,' the doctor said.

'I wonder how much I weigh? It must be minus figures by now.'

'Only one way to find out.' The doctor pointed at the scales; which had been returned to their rightful place in the corner of the room.

Joe looked at them suspiciously. Then he straightened his back, walked over and mounted. To his relief the dial began to rise. It stopped at 12 stone 2 pounds. He shook his head in disbelief and began to laugh. All the while tears ran down his cheeks.

'What's all this noise?' said Anne from behind them.

Joe proudly displayed his new body to her.

'Oh my gosh. Is that really you?'

'All 12 stone and 2 pounds of me.'

'His optimum weight,' the doctor added.

Anne wrapped her arms all the way around him for the first time since they had been teenagers and they kissed

'I've decided something,' Jo said.

'What?' Anne asked.

'To leave Weeton.'

'Do you really mean it this time?'

'Oh yes, I've got big plans for us, little lady.'

She gave him a huge kiss.

The doctor coughed. 'Well I best be going.'

The pair thanked him all the way to the front door.

'We will miss you,' the doctor said.

'We have to go,' they said.

'I know.'

'Goodbye, Paul,' Joe said.

'Goodbye, Joe. Just remember there's only one real solution to being overweight.' He poked Joe's belly. 'And that is to eat less.'

When It Will Be Over

GALATIA GRIGORAKI

My American lover said,
'Your fantasy is impossible,
a masterpiece.'

I moved here,
thinking it,
the land of,
the possible…

Thank you,
I answered,
to his disembodied voice over the net.

He sent one picture,
precisely two.

Looked handsome in the first,
in the second he looks real.
Like a man,
who needs to be loved.
Over and over and over again
and again.

I responded.

'My marital status will chase you away,'
he argued
next,
he was making love to me,
a masterpiece.

Neither could see,
the other.

'When it will be over … '
he uttered,
but did not finish,
the sentence.

Instead he forgot his keys,
to the house where he lives,
with his wife.

I love her already,
with murderous envy,
since he does.

When it will be over,
I could visit his house
and roll around in the mud with his kids,
we could bathe in the garden tub in summer,
make snowmen in the yard in winter,
be allowed to send him birthday presents in the post.

We won't have to 'steal',
together time.

When it will be over,
his wife may know me,
as a friend.

Will we still want to fall into bed?
like the first time...

The first time,
blindfolded next to a stranger,
terrified.

Face under a pillow,
only the smell of his skin,
to reassure me,
then he took my hand and kissed it.

When it will be over,
we will still dream,
the same old impossible fantasies,
and hang them from the walls,
like freshly washed and ironed poems.

Ready for us to dress ourselves in,
and walk out,
into the 'real' world,
of masterpieces?

When it will be over,
I will have taken him home,
to the wilderness.

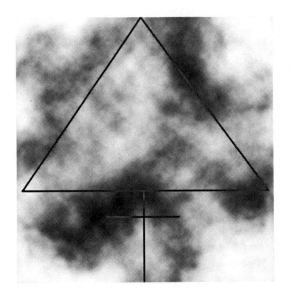

The Life Of The Mind

SUE LANZON

*This is the first of two extracts from **Something In The Water**, a collection of stories taken from the real life and work of a contemporary homeopath. Written in the first person, these stories offer an insight into the principles and practice of homeopathy, removing the veil which hovers between the more arcane aspects of a two-hundred-year-old, poorly understood medical system and life at the sharp end of the 21st century inner city.*

Courtauld Institute, The Strand. My friend, Jessie, has dragged me here for a lecture on D. H. Lawrence, given by a writer she greatly admires. She admired his last book so much that she decided, on turning the last page, she wanted to marry him.

'I feel I need a writer in my life,' she says.

'Why?'

'Because...' She pauses outside the Courtauld entrance and looks skyward as the first few flakes of snow arrive with us at the threshold leading to the Royal Society Of Literature,

'...because I want to be written.'

Inside, I play Spot The Critical Theorist as the lecture hall fills. I notice I've already started thinking in Upper Case.

'I don't, in fact, know the first thing about D.H. Lawrence,' Jessie says, suddenly peering into the abyss of her own ignorance.

'I don't either,' I lie, as The Writer arrives. A tall, skinny, dishevelled aesthete with a large red nose and a chaotic sheaf of notes, he clears his throat and furrows his extremely high and pimply brow, '...but your husband-to-be probably knows enough for all of us.'

'Sssh,' a woman behind me hisses intellectually, as The Writer begins.

The man sitting on my right has an odour redolent of decades of literary struggle in un-aired, dusty rooms. My chair is uncomfortable. I have a great view of the back of someone's head and amuse myself for a few nanoseconds by diagnosing her current health problems from the texture of the skin on her neck and the position of her right shoulder. It's a thing we complementary therapists do in idle moments when there are no copies of the Times Literary Supplement to peruse. It's called reading the body.

The Writer is droning on in a vainglorious, bombastic sort of way about the demise of the Novel of Ideas. I find myself anticipating my snowbound journey home courtesy of South East Trains, and decide I'd better have a couple of glasses of publishers' plonk before setting off.

Everyone else appears to be riveted. The air is rapt with Reverence for the Intellect. The Writer mentions loins at one point and my ears prick up momentarily, but the moment passes. I just want to Go Somewhere and Lie Down.

I slide further into my seat in order to become as horizontal as possible without actually collapsing onto the floor and, as I pass into an altered state one might call Literature Fatigue, I realise, too late, I'm succumbing to a room full of Sulphur.

Sulphur is known as the king of remedies. This is because, in its material state, it is responsible for producing approximately three thousand symptoms and therefore, according to the homeopathic principle of like curing like, is able in homeopathic doses to cure just as many. However, for the sake of brevity and to encapsulate its essence, Sulphur symbolises the point at which the mind created the delusion that it was separate from the body. In an evolutionary sense, this may be the point at which sickness began.

The typical Sulphur type is described as the 'ragged-trousered philosopher.' Prone to flexing the intellectual muscles at the expense of personal hygiene, Sulphur is also prone to, well, being prone. The favoured position is recumbent. The favoured pastime is theorising. The favoured sound is of their own voice. Physically, the action of Sulphur is centrifugal and, like the eruption of volcanic matter, it encourages toxins to rise to the surface and discharge. It's messy, itchy, smelly and usually very red. The Sulphur patient may have skin problems, lung problems, liver problems, bowel problems, sweat problems and, quite possibly, mental problems. As the energy concentrates itself in the intellect, the normal body processes suffer from inactivity and lack of reaction. As the brain gets over-loaded, there is a tendency to lose the thread and become absent-minded and eventually, paradoxically, incapable of rational thought.

The homeopathic world is full of Sulphurs. They are the ones doing all the research, writing the books, trying to explain to those of us who are just doing it anyway how homeopathy works. They are the ones giving over-priced seminars on why their particular method of prescribing is the one that will revolutionise my practice. They are the ones spending entire afternoons in online chat groups debating the optimum diameter of a sugar dragee. They are the ones who encourage dogma in an attempt to make the world fit in with their systems, their theories, their ideas. The fact that this is often at the expense of the patient's well-being is irrelevant to them.

Samuel Hahnemann, the founding father of homeopathy and therefore, inevitably, Sulphur to the core, once exhorted us all to "Have no theories." I like the barefaced cheek of this, and it endears Sam to me, despite my having to acknowledge that it is, in itself, a theory.

The lecture has finished. It's Q&A time. The audience now recognises its chance to shine yet there are no real questions posed to The Writer, more a series of pretentious comments from the floor regarding abstraction, social delineation, radical verse-forms, and a spirited defence of the misogyny which pervades Lawrence's work.

Jessie's muttering something about deciding not to mix her gene pool with The Writer's after all. I tell her she never had a chance anyway, not with all these publishing maidens gagging for a quick one in the foyer, and suggest we just make for the exit and be first in line for the plonk. I can tell by her lack of reaction that she's disappointed, both in The Writer and in me. We don't fit with her idea of how it's meant to be. I want to cheer her up so I seize the moment and, rousing myself from my position halfway under the chair, wave my fist in the air and cry, 'Better Passion and Death than any more of these Isms!' There is a shocked silence as I grab Jessie and we slither cravenly towards the door.

'What came over you?' she says, once we're downstairs, clutching cheap Rioja in our red sweaty paws. 'I never knew you could be, like, that embarrassing.'

'It's a quote...from Lawrence...as in D. H. I was being clever, actually.'

In an attempt to distract her, I point towards the window. 'Look! Outside. It's beautiful.'

We crunch our way down a silvery Strand arm-in-arm, the intense cold annihilating the sulphurous fumes still emanating from the Courtauld, the snow like a blank sheet of paper inscribed with our footprints, letting us make our mark on the world.

'Here's another quote for you,' I offer. ' "The wise man believes in nothing." '

'Who said that?'

'It doesn't matter.'

'Courtauld. Caught cold. Think I'll catch a bus instead,' she says, giggling at her own wit and brilliance.

Better than being caught napping, I think lazily as I trundle towards Charing Cross, my breath leading the way home in swirling hicroglyphs, like snowflakes, impossible to pin down.

Searching

FERDI MEHMET

'You've gotta do things properly,' said Harris. 'You ever get married, she's gotta be average, or below. Don't marry a stunner.' He was about to drink, paused. 'You'll regret it for the rest of your life.'

Harris and I were having a drink to celebrate my new job at the library. I told him I had no intention of marrying and he laughed. He even attempted eye contact with the barman, to invite him in on the joke.

'Look, Nelson,' said Harris. 'You're barely, what, twenty-two years old? By the time you're my age, you'll have had your heart ripped out and crushed a few times, and at least once,' he pointed to me to emphasize his point, 'you'll walk in on your woman doing the dirty with some hotshot, big-head, small-dick city-worker, and you know what she'll do? She'll look you square in the eye and deny everything. Even as the guy is zipping up and winking at you, she'll tell you you're nuts, paranoid, make you think *you're* the problem. And if you're not careful, you'll be on your knees apologizing to *her*.'

Harris Osborne was a fifty-eight-year-old English teacher and novelist. He mainly wrote romance and erotic fiction. He'd never married, and had no children. I was Harris's student once, that's how we met. One break-time I was smoking a joint in the car park and Harris sniffed it out like a police dog.

What is that, hash?' he said.

I nodded. 'You won't tell anyone, will you?'

'Not if you give me a drag.'

Harris went on to tell me how much cannabis and its culture had changed since he was a young man.

'Nowadays, people wanna stuff three grams of bionic high-grade skunk into a joint and swim into oblivion,' he said. 'That's not what it's about. It's about relaxing with your chums, talking, indulging in the music. It's a journey you take.'

I admired Harris. Certainly he had a screw loose, but he was a good man. And there was usually great logic in his madness. Once we were in a bar in Central London. It was busy and one of the barmen took Harris's drink, thinking it was finished.

'Excuse me,' said Harris. 'I wasn't finished with that.'

The barman looked at the glass, which was now grouped with several dirty glasses.

'Sorry,' he said, and placed the drink back in front of Harris.

'Er, you stuck your fingers in my drink,' said Harris.

'What?' The barman smiled.

'What's funny?'

'Look, I made a mistake,' said the barman. 'Your glass was next to those dirty ones Phil put on the bar.'

'It was your mistake,' said Harris. 'I shouldn't have to pay for it.'

The barman seemed to cheer up. 'Can I get you another drink?'

'No, thanks,' said Harris. 'It was an honest mistake.'

The barman looked puzzled and walked away.

'You see, Nelson? People will always try to take the Mick. You have to stand firm and show you won't accept it.'

I nodded, unsure of what just happened.

'It was never about the drink,' said Harris. 'It's about general decency, and doing the right thing. Sure, it was an error, but that man insulted me. So he should respect me as a fellow human being and offer to make amends.'

'But you turned down the drink.'

'That's right,' said Harris. 'The important thing is he made the offer. That's all I wanted, not a free drink, but some respect for the customer who pays his wages.'

We drank late into the evening. Harris was starting to relax.

'What about your book?' He smiled. 'The great *post*-post-modern novel that'll change the world.'

I'd been talking about writing that novel for years. I just didn't know where to start, and when I did have a crack, a day's work would end up in the bin. I couldn't find my feet. That was the other reason I respected Harris. He'd written twenty-nine novels already, and number thirty was almost complete.

'I don't have the discipline,' I told him.

He waved that away. 'You don't have the guts, more like,' he said, his eyes struggling to focus. 'You spend too much time thinking, and not enough time doing. Maybe it's connected to your fear of being alone.'

'Well... what about you, Harris? What's your secret?'

'Me?' he said. 'There's no secret. I've been writing the same novel for twenty-five years. Romance and sex, my friend. That stuff - the sex... It's the most basic human drive. What else is there? I mean what is the real reason you wake up in the morning? Because your dick tells you to. And it promises you the possibility of coitus if you get dressed and leave the house. Guys without dicks are not happy bunnies.'

He laughed.

'What about women?' I said.

'Women?' He perked up. 'Nothing but blokes with complications. And without the penis, of course. Which, frankly, I think they're rather envious of.'

And that was when I saw her. She was sitting by the window, talking with another young woman. I stared, and we made eye contact. A few seconds later she looked again, and so did her friend. They started to get up.

'Harris, those women,' I said. 'I think they're coming over.'

Harris stole a look. 'Not bad. If they want you to take them home, make sure they don't tie you up or place you in any other difficult situations.'

I looked at him. 'What kind of life have you lived, Harris?'

'Hi,' said the attractive one, reaching for Harris's hand. 'I'm Sam Green. This is Rose Coleman.'

They all shook hands. Apparently I was invisible.

'You look familiar,' Harris told Sam. 'I think I've seen you around.'

'Oh, I'm a big fan, Harris,' said Sam. 'That whole *Eliza* series - just brilliant.'

Harris looked at me and scratched his head. 'That's great. Uh, this is my young friend, Nelson White.'

They smiled and nodded.

'Let us buy you guys a drink,' said Rose.

The first bottle of red was followed promptly by another.

Sam was fixed on Harris, drowning in his mere presence.

'You can get away with all that emotional turmoil if you use a female character,' said Harris. 'With a man it would be hard to forgive, that readiness to destroy, the lack of order.'

The spell was broken.

'Readiness to destroy?' said Sam. 'Lack of order? Is that how we are?'

Harris held his hands up. 'You have to be authentic. Or you'll be labelled a charlatan.'

He smiled, looked at me, then started to pull himself out of his chair.

'As fun as this little interview is,' he said, 'I have to go. I want at least an hour of sleep. Early start.'

'Okay, Harris, you take care.'

He waved and walked away, out of the bar and onto the street. He grinned at me as he slid out of view.

Sam and Rose turned to me.

'He's a good guy,' I said.

'Do you like Sting?' said Sam.

'Sting?' I said.

'Yes, Sting. The musician.'

'Uh. No. No, I hate Sting. I actually *hate* Sting.'

And that was how I met Sam Green.

Within a week we were having the greatest sex of my life.

Within a month I was living with her.

My day at work was a breeze, as usual. At seven o'clock I was ready to pick up some food and go home.

Harris phoned me as I stepped into the Chinese restaurant.

'Nelson,' he said. 'Still alive?'

'Harris, what's up?'

'Where are you?' he said.

'About to order food, actually.'

The girl behind the counter was waiting. I held a finger up.

'Can you come to The Bell?' said Harris.

He sounded nervous.

'Um...'

'For god's sake, man.'

'All right, I'll... I'll be down in a minute.'

I told the girl I'd be back later and took a walk to the pub.

When I arrived, Harris was sitting by the entrance waiting for me.

'About time,' he said.

'It's been two minutes,' I said, and sat down opposite him.

There was a pint of cider waiting for me. I took a sip and eyed Harris. He was rubbing his forehead, and there were three empty pint glasses in front of him.

'What's happened?' I said.

He looked around the pub, which was filling up, then looked at me. 'I might be having a midlife crisis.'

I arrested my initial desire to laugh. 'You're fifty-eight,' I said.

Harris was affronted by this. 'What does that mean?'

'Well, midlife, er...crisises?'

'Crises,' he said.

'Yeah, those. Don't they usually happen...well, midlife?'

He leaned back, staring at me, shaking his head. 'Let me tell you something, Nelson. I had my first midlife crisis at the age of eighteen.'

Now I laughed and relaxed a little.

'It's true,' he said. 'I'd written one book already, and had the love affair of a lifetime with an experienced older woman, *and* had it all fall apart on me.' He held his hands open. 'What was I to do?'

I took a mouthful of cider.

'You still seeing that feminist?' he said.

'Who, Sam? Yeah. Yeah, um... I'm still... Sorry, feminist? Not sure that's accurate.'

Harris waved it away. 'How are things?'

'Good. We're doing well.'

That was mainly true. Sam could get paranoid from time to time, though. I didn't feel like telling Harris that.

He smiled. 'I'm glad. Enjoy these times, Nelson. Enjoy your youth and the endless possibilities that go with it.'

I leaned forward.

'Okay, Harris, what the hell are you talking about? Hmm? Are you dying or something? You're not dying, are you?'

'No,' he said. 'I'm not dying. I don't think so.'

'Then what's up with you?'

He took a moment, then sighed. 'I woke up this morning, Nelson, and you know what I thought?'

I waited.

'I was shaving, looking at myself in the mirror, razor in hand, and suddenly...out of nowhere...I thought, *My god. I have everything.* Not a big bank balance or twenty-five houses and thirteen cars, I mean... I've got everything I need or want in life and there is nothing I feel deprived of.' He thought some more. 'And that took me fifty-eight years. My whole life to get to that stage. Some people never get there, you know.'

I watched him. 'This is a good thing, surely.'

He shook his head. 'It *was* a good thing, Nelson. It was the most beautiful feeling. I wasn't prepared for it, it blew my mind.'

I said nothing.

'But what follows the high of all highs?' He looked away. 'There's only one way to go after that.'

There was silence between us. I thought about what Harris was saying. 'So you reached a state of total contentment,' I said. 'The peak of your life, and… And it lasted just a few minutes?'

'Seconds,' he said.

'So how do you feel now?'

'Low, Nelson. I feel low.'

'But you just said, clearly, that you have everything you could want or need, right?'

'Right. So? Now what? Now that I'm there, what do I do?'

'Well, isn't just being there enough?'

'See?' He held a finger up. 'That's just it, Nelson. Being isn't enough. Life is a journey. If the journey ends… Well, you're as good as dead.'

I nodded.

'So what's the answer, Harris?'

'The answer? Okay, I know what you're thinking. I know what you're getting at. I should start something new, right? Create new goals for myself? Hmm?'

I smiled.

'What would be the point, Nelson? If I'm merely destined to end up right back here again, what would… you know?'

'Wow,' I said, and downed half a pint of cider in one go. 'Wow, Harris, I… I never really thought of it quite like that before.'

He nodded, pleased I was starting to understand.

'So the point is,' I said, thinking. 'The point is… Life is about the journey, right? So enjoy the journey.'

'No, no,' he said. 'I mean yes, but no. Just a journey? Isn't the point of a journey to get somewhere, college boy?'

'All right,' I said. 'No need for insults. Um, yes, yes, the point of a journey is to get somewhere.'

'But what's the point if the destination leaves you empty and un-fulfilled?'

'Empty and unfulfilled?' I said. 'That's some statement, Harris.'

He almost cracked a smile. 'Yeah, well… Maybe that was over-doing it a bit.'

I glanced at the clock behind the bar.

'Look, Harris. Maybe you're not picking the right journeys. Or the right destinations, or…whatever. You know? I mean it's not all bad, is it?'

He stared at me a moment longer, then finished his drink and gently placed the glass on the table.

'Yeah.'

'I, uh… I should go, Harris. You want to meet tomorrow?'

Nothing.

'Harris? Drinks tomorrow?'

Another moment, then:

'Uh, yeah, yeah. Tomorrow. I'll bring those books you wanted.'

He stood up, took a breath, and headed slowly to the bar.

The following day, I arrived home from work.

'Where have you been?' said Sam.

She was sitting on the kitchen stool when I walked through the front door. Staring, smoking, waiting. The TV was off, so something was wrong.

'Sam. What's up?'

'What's up? It's nearly eight o'clock, Nelson.'

'Yeah, sorry. There was an accident on the road.'

'You're seeing someone, aren't you?'

I laughed. 'Sam, I'm fifteen minutes late.'

'Just admit it, Nelson. I've known for some time.'

I picked the kettle up, filled it with water and started to prepare a cup of coffee.

'Well?'

'Look, Sam. Do you honestly believe that I'm screwing around behind your back?'

Her face said she didn't. '…Maybe.'

'Do you want a coffee?'

'Don't change the subject.'

She shot up and started pacing the kitchen.

'Last week, in the Chinese restaurant, you were drooling all over those waitresses.'

'What?'

'Every time they walked by,' she said.

'So I was looking around the place,' I said. 'I was enjoying my meal, and the company I was in, and I was occasionally noticing the other human beings that were around. I wouldn't call it drooling all over them, Sam.'

The kettle was still boiling, so I reached for the sugar in the cupboard and placed it by the cup, just for something to do.

'What about the woman in the mobile phone shop?' said Sam, stubbing her cigarette. 'You couldn't stop looking at her.'

I stared at Sam.

'You mean the sales girl?' I said, 'Who worked in the shop, who was trying to sell me a phone?'

She walked away, opened a cupboard, grabbed a packet of cigarettes, and headed for the balcony.

'You always have an excuse,' she said.

My brain was starting to hurt.

I fixed my coffee, picked it up, took a deep breath and stepped out to join her.

'Sam - '

'Don't, Nelson. I don't know why you're even pretending to want me.'

I went to take her hand, but thought better of it.

'Look, Sam. I thought everything was okay now. Where's this come from?'

She took a drag of her cigarette and looked at me.

'Why are you with me?' she said.

I tried to look sincere. 'Because I want to be.'

'It's only going to get worse,' Harris told me, over drinks at The Bell. 'Personality Disorders. Ever heard of those? Every time you forgive her attacks on your loyalty, she'll go away with more ammunition, and each time the damage will be much worse.'

'You can't know that,' I said, staring at my beer bottle.

'Oh, but I do know that, young ignorant one.'

'Hmm. You seem a lot happier, Harris.'

'Yeah, well. I've been doing some thinking,' he said, looking around at the groups of people. 'It's time I walked over to the edge, took a deep breath, felt the fear, and made one gigantic leap.' He sipped his drink. 'I'm going to perform a bungee-jump.'

'A bungee-jump, Harris?'

'To start with. I was going to make more plans but I thought I'd wait and see if I... you know, survive.' He laughed.

'A bungee-jump,' I said. 'That's such a cliché.'

'Everything's a cliché,' said Harris. 'Everything.'

He then produced a small tobacco tin, opened it to reveal a lumpy white powder. He pinched a little and sniffed it.

'Ah, that's the stuff,' he said.

'Harris, is that coke? You're doing coke in the middle of the pub?'

He shrugged.

'I thought you didn't touch that stuff anymore. Since it made you, you know, nearly stab your father.'

'Life is short,' he said. 'Plus, my father's dead. Thank goodness. But back to Sam.' He sniffed. 'Trust me, Nelson. This is the beginning of the end for you. A very long and bitter end, if you don't retreat soon.'

'Well. I mean she seemed okay after our chat,' I said.

'Of course she did. For now. Shall we get some wine?'

'What do you mean, for now?'

'What it means is... Sam has now seen how easily she can manipulate you. You've forgiven her. Just like that. And you know what? Secretly - she'll never admit to this - but secretly she enjoys her control over you and the suffering she causes, and - I'm sorry, Nelson - she loathes you for it. That's the sad truth, my friend. Now finish up.'

I finished off my bottle.

'She loathes me for it?'

'Well, yes. She doesn't want a man who can't stand up for himself. Especially against a petite little mouse-bitch like her. I fancy chilled rosé. It's a warm night.'

'Yeah, okay, I'll go.' I stood up and pulled my wallet from my pocket. 'So... What should I do, Harris?'

'Hmm? Oh, well… Really, you should stand firm and tell her it won't do, that you won't put up with it.'

I thought about it and shook my head. 'Why is this so complicated?'

'Welcome to the world of crazy women, my friend. Enjoy that recent memory of the easy life. Because it's packing its bags and going bye-bye.'

I noticed the bar was quiet now, a good time to order the wine.

'Harris,' I said. 'Why? What does Sam actually want from all this…crap?'

He looked me in the eye for the first time.

'Honestly?' He took a moment. 'Probably because she wants out.'

'She - '

'Wants out, yeah. Some people, it's just easier to fight their way out, making a big mess as they do it, than it is to… well, than it is to talk about it, and be honest.'

I looked at the bar. A crowd was forming.

'I'll get us that wine,' I said.

I don't usually go home for lunch, but I had a few hours to spare, so I popped in to pick up my magazines.

And that's when it happened. I opened the front door and immediately I knew something was wrong.

There was a guy. He looked familiar. He stepped back against the kitchen cupboard, relaxing his hands, watching me.

Sam picked up the kettle, played with her hair, looking at me too.

'Nelson,' she said. 'You never come home at lunch. You okay?'

I looked at the guy. It was Martin-Something. He tried to look casual, sizing me up.

'Hi,' he said.

'You remember Martin,' said Sam. 'He was at Rose's party.'

The kettle was on the boil. The two of them stood opposite each other, a large kitchen space between them. They looked unnatural.

Uncomfortable.

'What's going on?' I said.

'What do you mean?' said Sam, and turned her back to reach for some cups. 'You want some tea?'

She adjusted her shirt as she lined up three cups.

'I should go,' said Martin. 'I'm meeting some friends.'

'Don't leave on my account, Martin. The two of you, just pretend I'm not here.'

Martin looked at Sam. Sam gave me a hard look.

I held my hands up. 'Come on. You were having a great time till I arrived, right? Is it me? Shall I leave?'

'Look, mate,' said Martin. 'I don't want to be in the way here.'

He started for the door. I should have grabbed him. I should have forced him to talk, to get on his knees and beg for mercy. I shouldn't have let him slide past me and out the door.

'You see?' said Sam. 'You scared him away.'

'Did I?'

'He's a good guy. So you do want tea?'

'No,' I said. 'I don't want tea.'

She carried on as normal.

'What was he doing here?'

'Hmm?'

'You heard the fucking question, Sam, now answer it.'

'Why are you shouting?'

'Because you're… You're all… You know why!'

Breathe, I thought. *Just breathe.*

'Sam. Answer the question. What - '

'What was he doing here?' she snapped. 'He was just, you know, he came by. He was on his way to The White Horse to meet his friends, and he dropped in. He's done it before. No biggy.'

'Oh, he's done it before?'

She continued preparing her tea. She poured the hot water, as calm as she always had.

'What are you getting so worked up about?' she said, looking a little angry now. 'Eh, Nelson? What are you saying?'

I looked at her.

'I mean, Jesus Christ, Nelson. How about a "Hi, Sam. Lovely to see you"? I mean, I've been feeling sick all day. You knew I wasn't well when you left. I've had my mum on the phone giving me a hard time about absolutely everything...' She stopped, looked down, took quick, sharp breaths. 'I mean, you know. I just want some comfort right now. Not an argument with a paranoid boyfriend.'

She shook her head, refusing to look at me. Then she picked up her tea, stormed off, and settled down on the sofa. She still had that hard look on her face.

'Um. Have I done something wrong?' I said, trying to sound neutral, without sarcasm.

She just sipped her tea.

'Oh, god,' said Harris. 'And then she wouldn't let you touch her in bed?'

'I... I never said that, did I?'

'No, you didn't,' he said. 'But that's what happened, right?'

'Well - '

'I knew it.'

Harris shook his head and continued to read his printouts as he spoke.

'If you don't see the signs now, Nelson, you may well be doomed for the rest of your life.'

I had another mouthful of beer. I was drinking faster than usual tonight.

'What are you reading, Harris?'

'This? Oh, this is something one of my students wrote. A short story that pretends to be a comedy-drama about family life, but it's really about the horrors of fascism in a world struggling to be liberal. And the hypocrisy of everybody involved. Including, I should say, the author himself. It's not bad.'

The next day my decision was made. I was going to leave Sam. It wasn't an easy choice. But there was no light at the end of this tunnel.

I had to be strong for once.

I waited for Harris at The Bell. He was twenty minutes late, which was unusual. I called him for the second time, and, as I held the phone to my ear, he walked in. He was limping, his face bruised.

He smiled and nodded when he saw me.

'Harris?' I rose to my feet. 'What the hell happened to you?'

'Evening, Nelson.'

He gave me a soldier's salute and tried to pull the chair out, squinting as he did it. He managed to position himself over the seat and let himself drop.

'Ooh, god. Whoo! I tell you, Nelson... You know you're getting old when you have to make a noise to sit down.'

He reached for the cider I'd bought for him, struggled to bring it to his lips, took a sip.

'And what are all these kids doing here? Past their bed time, isn't it?'

'Harris, what the hell?'

He looked at me. 'Some guys mugged me last night.'

'My god.'

He shook his head. 'No, no, it wasn't all bad. I gave them a run for their money. Or, *my* money. I put up a good fight, Nelson, let me tell you.'

'You fought them?'

'Of course,' he said. 'I managed to get a few punches in, too.'

I couldn't believe what I was hearing.

'As you can see, they scored a few points. They were just standing there,' he said. 'Right next to a parked car. So I'm approaching them, and they've seen me, and I knew. Right then I knew. So one of them says, "Alright, granddad? Give us some pocket money." So I said, "Go and fuck your mother. See if she'll give you some money."'

'You are joking,' I said. 'You didn't say that.'

'What's mine is mine,' said Harris. 'You let people walk all over you, you'll die in shame, Nelson.'

'Harris- '

'So anyway, one of them punched me to the ground, then started going through my pockets. So I grabbed his arm and bit it.'

'You bit his arm?' I said.

'Yes, I bit his arm. Let me remind you, Nelson, that these men were assaulting me for money. I think that rather overshadows the fact that I sunk my teeth into their flesh.'

I was horrified. Yet a part of me wanted to laugh.

'That's when they all joined in. In the end they took my cash and left. I'm glad I did it, though, Nelson. Made me feel alive. I'd do it again.'

'My god, Harris,' I said. 'Did you go to the police?'

He scoffed. 'The police? What are they gonna do? No, they aren't interested in catching petty criminals.'

I eyed Harris up and down, shaking my head. 'You been checked out?'

'No,' he said. 'Anyway, forget that. You grown the balls to walk away from that life-sucking girlfriend yet?'

I sat back with my drink.

'Actually, no, *but*... I'm going to. I'm going to tell her soon. That's it. It's over. She was supposed to be visiting her mum this evening, but... Well... On the way here I saw her leaving The B-Line with some guys and girls. That Martin was with her, they looked pretty close.'

Harris sat back, creasing his face in pain.

'Glad to hear it,' he said. 'That you're planning to leave her, I mean. It'll be the best decision you've made this year. And remember, Nelson: the right thing to do is usually the hardest.'

I nodded.

'So, I've got a big sky-diving weekend coming up,' he said.

'What? You're not still going through with that?'

'Of course,' he said. 'If they let me. And in a few weeks, I think I'm gonna take off. Travel around Europe. Smoke some opium. Write my next book while I'm on the road. Something different this time. Less lovey, more...real. But we'll see.'

I wasn't sure if he was serious. 'You're leaving?'

'Only for a short while. Maybe it will help me cope with these thoughts I've been having, and inspire me to take the next big step.

Whatever it is.'

A group of young guys walked in. They looked at me, then at Harris, and continued to the bar. I wondered, as I sometimes did: who were those people? Where had they come from, and where were they going? What would they be feeling in the cold early hours?

'What I've realized,' said Harris, 'and I knew this when I was younger, but the idea seems to grow with potency as I get older: life is fucking nuts. It's absurd. There's no right or wrong way. There just is what there is. You go searching for answers, the best you can hope for is that your brain will find a pattern of some sort in all the madness. Because that's what it does, the brain. It tries to find the pattern, the logic. But it's just an illusion.'

The bar was filling up now. Harris looked around.

'More often,' he said, 'There are no answers. You're in the picture house, and suddenly *boom*, the screen goes dark and the credits roll.'

I was deep in thought, but my laughter pulled me out. Maybe it was an uncomfortable laugh. I couldn't say.

My bag of clothes was packed, and my posters of Friedrich Nietzsche and Pink Floyd's *Dark Side of the Moon* were rolled up under my arm.

Sam walked in as I buttoned my jacket.

'It's true?' she said. 'You're really leaving?'

'Yes,' I said. 'Gonna stay with my parents until... Look, we both know - '

'You bastard,' she said.

'Me? You've been screwing around, lying to me, Sam.'

She stormed past me and into the bedroom.

'You know my sister called?' she said.

I waited a moment. 'And?'

She appeared at the bedroom door.

'Heart attack, Nelson. My dad. He's in hospital.'

She started to fill up, backed away into the room.

'Shit,' I said. 'Is he okay?'

'He's had a fucking heart attack, moron, what do you think?'

I was still. I couldn't think. This wasn't right.

'Are you still here?' she said.

'Um. Yeah. I don't have to go.'

'Get the fuck out of my life!' she screamed. 'Go live with your alcoholic, loser parents. And tell your boyfriend, Harris Osborne, his books are shit.'

I gently closed the door on our life together.

When I made it to the street, I saw the group of young guys from the pub. I stopped, put my bag down to phone a cab, and they walked past me. One of them stared an extra second.

As I searched for the number of the cab service, my phone rang. PRIVATE NUMBER.

I answered it.

'Nelson White?' said a voice.

'Yes?'

She took a moment. 'My name is Amanda Roberts, I'm calling from North Middlesex Hospital. Harris Osborne has you listed as a contact in case of emergency. You know Harris Osborne?'

Formative Friendships

BECCA LEATHLEAN

It's winter 1974 and I'm in the bathroom at 15 Methuen Street. The bathroom is downstairs, next to the kitchen, and the bath is filled with washing up. There's about two weeks' worth. I've lumped it all in together - greasy frying pans and china cups, knives and forks and beer glasses. I've squirted it with half a bottle of washing up liquid and turned on the hot tap. Now I'm kneeling on the floor, wiping the soapy crockery with a dishcloth and piling it up on the bathmat to dry.

It's my first visit to stay with my friend Suze and her mum in Southampton. We arrived half an hour ago. Suze unlocked the front door and called for her mum, and we tramped down the cold, damp corridor towards the kitchen.

Mari is at the kitchen table. She's slumped over it, droopy-drunk with a soggy Woodbine in her hand. She half-greets Suze and me, wheezes and looks vague. She's a tiny, bird-like woman, with short, straight yellow-and-black hair. She wears a long white cardi, black slacks and large, black-framed glasses. And she is surrounded by dirty dishes.

I don't think I've ever seen a drunk woman before.

My own mum got tiddly one Christmas, giggling on the way home from the village panto, saying that if anyone lit a match any-where near her mouth she might go up in flames. This is different. Suze is angry and, for once, lost for words. She stomps upstairs in some kind of confusion. And I, taking a look at the wreckage around me, decide the best thing I can do is wash up. It's good to be practical in these sorts of situations.

Suze and I are twelve. We go to a 'progressive' boarding school in Devon. Neither of us has the type of home-life that might imply. My dad is a judge in Hong Kong; hers is a Communist bus driver. Yet, birds of a feather, we are somehow drawn together. For me - naïve, withdrawn and awkward - she brings freedom. Racy, naughty, clever, gobby, she pulls me out of my shell and shows me another world.

A few weeks after we meet, we have a heart to heart in the bathroom. 'Is it the same thing with your mum as it is with mine?' she asks. I'm not too sure, so Suze plucks up courage to go first. Her mum is an alcoholic.

I don't know what to think. Truth be told, I'm shocked at the thought of my prim and proper mum as an alcoholic. I think I'm a bit jealous, too. If Suze's mum is an alcoholic, surely she can just stop drinking and she'll be OK? 'No, it's not the same,' I eventually say. 'But it may be similar. My mum is mentally ill.'

Me and Suze are cockney rebels. We follow the band of the same name. We also get drunk, smoke dope, bunk off classes, shoplift, hitchhike and run away. One day, we decide to skip double-maths and hitch to Southampton. We walk down to Staverton and get a ride to the A38. Almost immediately, we are picked up by a lorry driver. As we settle down in the cab, I can't quite believe what we're doing. The maths lesson is still going on, and here we are, bombing down the dual carriageway in a lorry! There's a shelf behind the seats for sleeping. Suze chats to the driver like a grown up. He doesn't pry - he treats us to a fry up in a motorway cafe and drives us 150 miles to our destination.

Mari is surprised when we knock on her door. More than that, though, she's sober and pleased to see us. She asks how my mum is and says I'm welcome any time. She phones the school to say we're safe. We'll have to go back tomorrow, but until then we'll have fun.

Mari is the opposite of my mum. She reads the *Morning Star*. She listens to Radio 1. She makes tea with teabags and toast out of white sliced bread. That evening she takes us to her local - a tiny front room of a pub with wooden benches around the walls. She buys cider for herself and Snowballs for us. She introduces her friends, Paddy and Tipperary Jock. We all smoke roll-ups. No one bothers about us being under age. This is a forbidden world yet I feel happier, safer, braver and more at home here than anywhere. Mari's teaching me something that will stay with me forever - you find kindness and generosity in the most unexpected places.

Peace with the Grotesque

MAXINE MCLEARY-JONES

A virtual paradise of comfort and joy
Limbs and fine fur sprouting with teeth budding
In perfect form
A tiny heart to break a few
An acid tongue from milky coos

Unimpeded growth with tides of sickness
Companions for nine months of a lifetime my dear
Waves of torture and undying despair
To be replaced by mummy's life giving elixir

Praise for the soft delicate bundle of baby.

How do pain and beauty coexist with such ease?
A worthy lesson for us all, as all is not as it seems.

What about the woman at the bus stop,
Summer dress and sparkly shoes?
Hair wrapped up in a ribbon and a flower adorning her bloom.

She turned round with a puff of smoke
So acrid you would really choke
A nasty cough from lungs so battered
'Please get a broom for that plume!'

Teeth matching the yellowing fingers
With a nicotine stained nail or two
What would mother say to that?
'Lawd mi God you see what cigarette can do!'

Or take the couple down the road
Mr and Mrs Perfection it would seem
Beautiful hanging baskets outside their front door
Front porch with such a gleam

Peek inside and see the crystal 40 inch colour TV
Only strange you would never see her
For many weeks at a time

'Was that really screaming we heard? Oh well never mind.'

Is the only comfort with the mother, tummy like warm jelly?
She would soothe a bucket load of tears
Shaking away those many fears.

Bruised knees and childish taunts become a distant memory
When mama gets to work those pains will definitely flee.

Her body has seen better days, properly stretched, and worn
But that is her beauty, a wonderful confection of spiritual form.

Love, laughter, life itself along with strong, stony stare
It is all the nourishment we needed, our forebears would swear.

Strawberry smile with gentle hand, her gorgeous comforting embrace
Rice and peas on a Sunday for a generation free of chains.
Seeds of life, watered and grown, plenty hugs along the way
Their roots deserve to be revered, without them the soul would stray.

Teardrops of wisdom handed down
The throne will certainly be theirs
Love and laughter is their manna, guiding the way towards the upper stair.

Keep in mind the light ahead
Etched within eternal memory
The karmic bonds will set you free
Close your eyes wide open, tight, to see.

The Sydenham Ladies' Society

KATE ROSE

*The following chapter is taken from the novel **The Hidden Phases
of Venus**. Spanning the 1860s through to the present day, it unravels
the quests of two women, whose lives become intimately linked, as
they attempt to reconcile freedom, love and art.*

*'Mrs Ballinger is one of the ladies who pursue Culture in bands,
as though it were dangerous to meet it alone'.*
                                                      Xingu, **Edith Wharton**

May 31ˢᵗ, 1861

The Sydenham Ladies' Society for Cultural Studies - of which I
am a loyal member - gathers at the Crystal Palace on the last day of
each month, excepting the Sabbath. Today, as I struggled with the
wretched turnstile, a group of nearby gentlemen passed a communal
smirk. I thought: let them look; how ridiculous to reveal chinks in
their armour over a pair of ankles! Besides, whose fault was it:
mine for my lack of ladylike carefulness, or theirs for their vulgar
curiosity?

One and ten widows and myself meet by the Fancy Manufactur-
ers display. *En masse,* we move slowly toward the Dining Room in
the South Transept. Most are hard of hearing. I invariably have to
slouch to avoid shouting; pace reduced to a slow shuffle. Through
virtue of age and the Queen Mother's death having past its sixth
week, I am the only one not consigned to wear black. I have be-

come, one might say, the colourful plumage at the head of a dark, meandering reptile.

'You are speaking today, are you not?' said Mrs Copeland, a collector of fine Renaissance art.

I explained I had chosen to speak about 'The Greatness of Art'.

'I am keen to hear your views, my dear.'

'My own and Mr Ruskin's,' I replied, omitting to mention Father's reluctance to lend the critic's essays, believing ladies with adequate homes in which to entertain had no need to congregate in public places. There was, of course, every need.

We paid at the kiosk and were shown to our seats by a waiter with a twitching left eye. He assembled a crude circle, and after much repetition, took our orders for tea. At four o'clock, the room echoed with the insistent yet comforting trill of cutlery against crockery. A nearby hound yelped in its sleep. An elderly waiter chased away street urchins, flapping a towel as though swatting a fly.

My glances to this wider world were made surreptitiously, the other members not sharing my enthusiasm for humanity. Rather, they gathered for cake, or because the scarcity of visitors has left them with surplus time on their hands. Respectfully, they profess motives of a cultural nature. They read fervently - on a variety of subjects yet… yet somehow their opinions flutter like feathers upon a surface of a pond. I, meanwhile, drink up this wider world as if parched. It nourishes, yet does not satisfy. I may well have consumed seawater; such is my thirst for more.

I talked about how the greatest art conveys to mind the greatest number of ideas, trying not to be put off by the eleven unsmiling, unimpassioned faces. I finished. They politely applauded. Mrs Patterson gathered the slackened reins of conversation, claiming the speech *dee-light-fowl*; asked if there were any questions. Unsurprisingly, there were none.

After a lengthy rummage in her basket for a book, which she waved about with great enthusiasm, Mrs Patterson said shrilly, 'Mr

Darwin's, *On the Origin of Species by Means of Natural Selection* - I would like to know if it is literature, or simply science?'

'Poetry,' said Mrs Edge, a frail lady in a spidery shawl.

'Poetry, ah! Then I beg of you listen,' said Mrs Patterson, licking a finger, thumbing through pages. 'Whilst travelling on the omnibus here, I read a passage in which Mr Darwin compares affinities of beings to a tree. He said - where are we now? - yes, here it is: "...I believe it has been with the Great Tree of Life, which fills with its dead and broken branches the crust of earth, and covers the surface with its ever branching and beautiful ramifications."' Mrs Patterson studied our faces. 'Well?' she said, 'Does it not bring tears to one's eyes?'

'He refers to the Family Tree. But whose?' said Miss Soames, between mouthfuls of teacake.

'Man's a heathen!' Mrs Ash tapped out syllables upon the floorboards with her cane. 'He calls the works of God mere mockery and deception. Heathen, I tell you!'

'It is just as I said,' bellowed Mrs Edge, deafer than most. 'Poetry. A Divine Comedy of sorts. I should say the chap's imagination is far from lacking.'

At times I suspected these women of possessing more than a withered kernel of artistry themselves. I had reached the fourth chapter of Mr Darwin's dreary book and encountered no such poetry. However, poetry of the richest kind was happening as we spoke: happening to the woman with the peacock feathers in her hat, plucking currants from her cake; happening to the gentleman making paper boats for his wide-eyed children; and to the young man gathering roses from a street vendor, thrusting them at his lady friend who awoke from her ennui to burst into sudden laughter.

'No religion at our meetings, Mrs Ash. Remember the rules.'

'And no wars either, Mrs Copeland. Yes, I know, I know,' said Mrs Ash snapping her fan shut. 'Therefore may I mention how disappointed I was about the withdrawal of funds from the Female School of Art?'

'A mere setback,' said Mrs Copeland. 'The School will...'

And obligingly they fluttered from Darwin to a society of which none are members but all dutiful visitors, and I found myself regarding a foreign girl. She was about my age, sitting opposite a distinguished gentleman. Her manner was frank, intense, punctuated by exaggerated actions like those of the Southern Europeans. The gentleman meanwhile observed her with the animation of coal. Such a waste of enthusiasm, I thought, whilst on the back of my speech - hardly aware of my actions - I began sketching the girl's hands; her long fingers and the neatness of bones about her neck. Too distant for exactness, I idly invented: shiny eyes, full lips, hair concealing parts of her face as if to hint at some deeper level of concealment.

'Whilst we harvest mere opinions, ladies, the artist amongst us creates!' declared Mrs Patterson, glancing over my shoulder, causing me to cease what I was doing. Moreover, I was given little choice; they requested the drawing be passed round, and I obliged, finding myself quite curious as to their responses.

'With just a few lines you have transcribed the essence of character,' said Mrs Copeland who dipped beneath the surface in the manner of a gull diving for fish. 'I stare not at a girl but at the spirit living within the girl. If I might say: just the sort of experience satisfying enough to convince one of the richness offered by the life of the senses. Do you not agree, Mrs Ash?'

I smiled appreciatively; if I had indeed captured the girl's essence, it had been passed from eyes to charcoal without analysis.

'Yes, she's a pretty young thing,' said Mrs Ash, bobbing up again upon the lake's surface. 'Reminds me of my son's second daughter, or is it his third?'

The drawing was returned. The couple had by this time vanished, replaced by a bloated gentleman devouring his ice-cream. I felt at a loss; regretted I had not had chance to finish my sketch. I closed my notebook and folded my hands neatly across its cover.

'You are really a very talented young lady,' said Mrs Patterson, ejecting the monocle from her eye. 'Perhaps you should consider exhibiting at The Female School of Art. Doubtless it could do with some support.'

I smiled with gratitude, being careful not to divulge my dreams in public. Such foolishness is to be reserved for one's journal.

'Female School of Art,' said Mrs Ash, 'tell me, is that the same as the Society of Female Artists?'

'Good Lord no Rachael, quite a different thing altogether!' replied Mrs Copeland.

'We all agree you should exhibit, dear,' said Mrs Patterson.

'The question is, what?' said Mrs Copeland, with a look that suggested she already knew.

Blushing, I studied the backs of my hands.

'And best not delay,' continued Mrs Copeland, 'or the matter of a husband will soon intervene.'

Teapots were emptied. Excuses were given: dressmaker appointments, Great Aunt duties, and benevolent acts of varying sorts, and we made our way through the Alhambra and Roman Courts, shuffling through Ancient Pompeii. Back at the Central Transept our farewells were, as usual, tediously drawn out.

It was as Mrs Edge exchanged culture for domestic gossip, expressing her delight over the employment of our previous parlour maid (Norah Baker was best known for sniffing the air like a mole), that an almighty crash echoed throughout the Transept, quickly followed by an almost inhuman screech barely distinguishable as, 'Testify to the Lord!' until it was repeated over and over, like a creature in the throes of death.

With much waving of her parasol, Mrs Ash summoned a guard. The young man with a red moustache explained how a young lady was affronted by the nude statuary.

'Do we know who she is?' said Mrs Ash in a conspiratorial tone.

'A convert of the Plymouth Brethren - so I'm led to believe,' replied the guard. 'She's knocked the statues' heads and arms clean off with her umbrella, Ma'am.'

We were herded to the nearest exit.

'Testify to the Lord!' once again bounced off the glass roof, hitting numerous organ pipes, and then we were outside, lifting our parasols and squinting against sunshine.

'She has every right,' said Mrs Ash.

'What do you mean *every right*?' said Mrs Patterson.

'Nudity is entirely unnecessary and female nudity in particular shames our sex!'

'Gracious Helen, you are as bad as the Bishops. I, for one, have nothing to be ashamed of.'

I covered my mouth in surprise. The Crystal Palace statuary - brazen or otherwise - had been previously ignored.

'Mrs Ash is always the most outspoken,' explained Mrs Copeland sidling up to me, taking hold of my arm. 'Lost her husband in the Crimean,' she added as if in explanation. 'Now I noticed, Miss Hamilton, if you do not mind me saying, how you agreed in your speech today with Mr Ruskin.' She abruptly stared toward the rose garden as if she had not spoken at all.

'I do indeed, Mrs Copeland,' I replied with certain pride - Mr Ruskin being the country's most respected critic.

'Then I assume you are not aware of Mr Ruskin's *personal* beliefs.'

'His personal beliefs, Mrs Copeland?'

'That a woman's intellect is not for creation but for - as he himself puts it - sweet ordering, arrangement and decision. I fear this does not match your own opinions, Miss Hamilton.'

'I had -'

'No, I thought as much.' She tapped my arm and released it. 'Nonetheless one ought to be aware of such views. We must, after all, know what men are assets to our cause and which are not.'

'I'm afraid -?'

'As Goethe puts it dear, "The little that is done seems nothing when we look forward and sees how much we have yet to do."'

With a lift of her parasol Mrs Copeland turned to Mrs Parker to continue a conversation about headless statues and the Plymouth Brethren. Bewildered, I slipped away.

Walking past the upper archery field, I considered Mrs Copeland's 'cause'. Could it be that Mr Ruskin's views about art were directed at men and men alone? Anyhow, I had little interest in the bureaucracy of painting - if such a thing existed. I wished to paint, that was all. I wished to embrace the Indian virtue of detachment, avoid the tedious vortex of the practical. Causes, after all, were ugly, practical affairs. Art, on the other hand, transcended the mundane. Of course, Mr Ruskin must know that women are born for creating - that this is their gift. Most likely the idea frightens him, or worse arouses envy. Envy, after all, makes a man unpredictable, prone to conquering countries not his for the taking.

Archery arrows whistled through the air. Applause trickled as though it were free-flowing water. It seemed the centre of a target had been forcefully struck. Indignantly, I shielded myself with my parasol and continued walking purposefully toward the exit, walking as if I might never escape.

The turnstile once again jammed, flagrantly exposing my ankles. Though breathless from the walk, this time I enjoyed the experience. Perhaps it was the shocked looks upon peoples' faces: their wide eyes, their pursed lips reflecting deep disapproval. Instead of blushing, I found myself smiling, even lifting my skirts a little higher. I experienced a sensation not altogether dissimilar to when I painted a fly on an orange skin, added a dead petal to a vase of freesias. It was the expression of the unusual that excited, and if it shocked - I thought as I freed my cage and rearranged my skirts to conceal the offending objects - so be it, for to feel shocked was to know one was truly alive!

107

Heart

LYNSAY MACKAY

Kiara grabbed the branch above her head and pulled herself up. This high up, the view was no longer blocked by foliage. She shielded her eyes from the glare of the midday sun and scanned the area. Her vision was flooded with a barrage of greenery. There was very little around her that was not disguised by the thick jungle growth.

Her eyes finally caught what they sought and she called out that her sisters should head east. By the time she snaked down the tree, her tribe was already on the move.

She caught pace with a passing sister and, with well-practiced gestures, indicated to the other woman that it was ten minutes to their destination. Teal grinned and signed thanks before increasing her speed and letting out a race call. All of the nearby women responded and the game was on.

By the time Kiara reached the clearing sweat was running down her back and her face glistened. Teal looked as though she had been there all day, not a drop of sweat could be seen and there was barely a hair out of place.

'Well run, sister,' Teal said, touching two fingers to her forehead in a sign of respect, 'but you'll need *celerit* to beat me,' she added with a wink.

Kiara returned the show of respect. 'The Goddess will marry before I beat you, sister.'

The noise of a branch snapping was the only warning the women had before they came from the trees. The second or two that the tribesmen gained from surprise cost Kiara a finger and nearly an eye.

Channa had been further into the clearing than Kiara and being the most experienced, she recovered the fastest. Her double blades were drawn in an instant and dragged across the throat of the first assailant from behind; Kiara hadn't even made the call for trouble before blood sprayed her face in a macabre imitation of a fountain. The attacker attempted one last swipe in Kiara's direction before slumping to the ground at her feet. 'Well met, sister,' she said as she ripped the dead man's clothes to wipe the blood from her eyes.

Channa signalled for silence. Kiara and Teal responded instantly, falling easily into a fighting stance. The sound of battle was all around the clearing. The tall dark men of the southern tribes had hidden well for the ambush, but then they had fought fiercely for the tribeswomen's land for generations and they rarely underestimated them. Channa signed that they should remain together and follow her lead. She trotted silently into the edge of the jungle, allowing the sounds of steel-on-steel to guide her to their destination; mere seconds later they were upon a battle scene, one sister fighting for her life against three of the southerners. She was bleeding from a number of wounds and was not going to last much longer.

Fingers moved in a blur and the three separated to pursue their targets. Channa dispatched her man quickly and without fuss, her sword slicing through his spine and piercing a lung in one swift movement. The other two assailants never stood a chance. Kiara and Teal were wiping blood from their swords before they could even scream.

'Can you walk?' Channa signed the injured sister.

'I can fight,' was the reply but Channa didn't see it. She was staring down, puzzled at the steel blade protruding from her chest. Her attacker was dead before she hit the ground, Teal and Kiara both moved like quicksilver, swords puncturing his heart and lungs. His death did nothing to help Channa.

The three women keened; the sound terrifying and heart rending; as though ripped from their throats. They would return for the body but for now they would avenge their sister.

The queue snaked around a few of the huts, slowly getting shorter as men were presented to the Great Mother and rejected.

Anxiety painted the faces of those going in, relief on those coming out. Nobody knew where the chosen men went but everybody knew that none returned. The only living males who came out of the Tribes' lands were the squalling baby boys who were given to the village to raise once or twice a generation.

Parka and Huren talked to ease the tension, the noise of their voices and laughter seemed to disperse it but it reformed, palpable and oppressive into any silence that occurred.

'I saw you dancing with Ilya at the Moon Day Fair,' Parka said, giving his friend a gentle nudge in the ribs, 'It won't be long before you're of age and everyone has seen the calf eyes she gives you.' The implication was so obvious and the conversation so familiar, Huren sighed in exasperation.

'I am under no obligation to marry before I am twenty-five and do not think that a honey sweet smile and child-bearing hips will make me relinquish my freedom before that.' They laughed together as old friends do upon hearing the expected.

Parka had known his other half almost all his life and could hardly wait to come of age but Huren was considerably less enthusiastic. 'I try, Huren, I really try to understand you but it's like you're from another tribe, maybe another jungle.' The grin they shared confirmed that this too was ground much covered.

'Maybe I am,' Huren replied, 'Maybe I'll go searching on my big day to a tribe more suited to me.' There was jest in his tone but Parka's eyes still fell.

'Maybe you will,' Parka said despondently but Huren clipped his friend's shoulder with the back of his hand,

'Oh, do not sulk, brother,' Huren said, 'You know I'll never leave, nobody leaves.'

The queue was shorter now and it was Parka's turn to face the Great Mother. 'Good luck my friend,' Huren said as he affectionately patted Parka's shoulder. Parka entered. Huren could not have said how long Parka was in the ceremonial hut, but it seemed like days before he emerged glowing with relief and gratitude.

'Your turn, friend,' Parka said offering the same familial gesture that Huren had given him. Huren took a deep breath and went inside. Parka waited in the same state of worry that Huren had been in whilst he was being judged. The village elder eventually came out and announced that the men should return to their work or families; Parka knew then that he would never see his friend again.

Kiara was clad only in what the jungle offered. Her body was all hard edges, with none of the soft curves that women usually held with such pride. Huren was dressed similarly, though less lavishly, as was fitting.

Kiara smiled shyly at him and he smiled unsurely back. It was a great honour for his family that he had been chosen as tribute to the Tribe, but the secrecy and occasional brutality of the Tribe meant the Chosen were not always grateful.

Comprehension lit Huren's eyes as he realised that he was to be bonded. He relaxed a little but it was obvious that he was still nervous. 'I greet you as the other half of me.' Kiara said in the language of the village people.

Surrounded by tribe sisters he knew how he had to respond. 'I greet you as the other half of me.' His voice was hoarse but sweet. Kia found her cheeks heating of their own accord. It was said that the Great Mother was always right in her choices but few believed it. When the colour of his cheeks rose to match her own, all doubts were chased from her mind.

The Great Mother rose from her dais, a sturdy unadorned piece, worn smooth by the generations of woman who had graced it. A novice held an arm each and her apprentice watched from just behind.

'I have deemed you a match, you will be fruitful, my child,' she said before turning to him. She laid her two fingers upon his lips and then on his forehead. The same gesture was repeated upon Kiara before she took one hand from each of them and placed them together whilst her two novices bound them with strong hemp.

'You will serve as two halves of a whole until the sundown seven days from now. May the Goddess bless this union.' The Great Mother raised their bound hands into the air and the tribe sisters cheered. Petals rained down upon them, seemingly from the sky.

Huren's hand had been laid atop Kiara's in the binding and she felt a slight squeeze. She turned to face him and did what was the final expectation in the ceremony. On slight tip toe Kia kissed his forehead, his nose and finally his lips. 'Let this union be sealed.' He repeated the gesture and the line with only mild hesitation. It was a brush of flesh rather than a kiss of love or passion but no more was expected at this time.

The first week of bonding was done with good purpose. At no point was a person alone for seven full days and nights. Being bonded to a stranger was something that all tribeswomen knew might be asked of them. Over generations the process had been refined and if the sister had not killed the man after a week then the chances of a child being born were good.

'He is strange,' Kiara told Teal while taking a break from sparring.

'How so?' Teal asked

'He says many things I do not understand, he talks of worship without blood, of life without pain.' She thought for a moment about not telling Teal the last part, but Teal was her Tribe Sister, they had been hearth mates before Huren. 'He talks of the Tribe with fear.'

Teal was nodding her head as Kiara talked, 'I have long suspected such things sister; we are not understood by those we protect. But Huren is not just a villager, he is also a man. You are not expected to understand him, just to mate with him.'

Kiara nodded in response. 'You are right, I should be thankful that I neither find him repellent or uninteresting. He is a good talker. I will learn much from him I think.'

Teal looked horrified at the prospect, 'He is a man Kiara; you must never forget that.' The sentence was emphatic and brooked no argument; this lesson was taught to Tribeswomen from birth. 'Mate and breed sister, do not befriend, it can only end badly. Now; let's fight.'

She screamed throughout the birth. To embrace pain one had to respect and give it what it asked for. Its price was submission. Tribeswomen knew this from a young age. If screaming helped then you screamed, only during the pain though, the memory of pain should never evoke tears or screams; that was the foundation of fear and fear was not a quality the tribeswoman favoured.

It was a long time before Kiara's screams were joined by the agonising first breaths of her child. 'Channa is reborn,' the midwife said, raising a baby girl into the view of Kiara. It would be the only time she was acknowledged as the child's mother and she wept. Her eyes full of tears and her mouth full of whimpers she reached her hands out for her daughter. She didn't even notice how the women around her bowed and gently shook their heads.

Kiara headed to her marriage hut on the outskirts of the village, having just finished her shift at the nursing hut. All men were kept outside the main camp and all knew it was death to enter. They were kept busy with crafts that aided the tribe, weaving, mending and cooking were but some of many.

She entered through the door flap and Huren looked up from the bowl he was carving. 'How is our daughter?' he asked.

Kiara shot him a look of pure fury. 'She is not our daughter, Huren, she is The Tribe's daughter.' The fury fell away as fast as it had arrived. She felt suddenly deflated and empty. 'I'm sorry, Huren. I know how hard this is for you to understand and how much it hurts not to be allowed to see her but we've covered this before. It's for

114

the best that she does not know you. We are Tribe and Tribe have no male influence whilst growing up.' Her eyes appealed for him to be reasonable, 'It is our way.'

She went to him and held him in her arms. His body shivered against her and she felt the hot salty tears as they fell from his eyes. 'It is not the right way, Kia,' he breathed into her shoulder and surprisingly she found herself nodding agreement.

'I know, my heart, I know.'

Kiara gave birth to her second child when Channa was four. It was a boy and as was proper he was gifted to the village. A week after his birth they came for Huren and Kiara in the night.

Neither wore anything more than a blanket and they stumbled along the paths as their escort prodded them to speed. Huren was breathing heavily as they were brought to a halt at the entrance of the Great Mother's hut. Kiara was struggling for breath too but not from exertion.

'Enter,' called the voice of one of the Great Mother's novices. Huren caught Kiara's hand and they entered the Great Mother's hut, right in the centre of the camp.

'Daughter,' the Great Mother addressed Kiara without even acknowledging Huren's presence. 'To love one not of the tribe is treason. The crime of treason is punishable by death. You have birthed a boy child and the Goddess is willing to accept the exchange.' There was a sharp prick at the back of her neck and then only blackness.

Kiara didn't move when she regained consciousness. She felt groggy but thought there were no other side effects. Silent and motionless she listened. There were at least a dozen of her sisters breathing in rhythm with each other.

Although she hadn't moved she had only a few seconds to think before the novices announced her, 'She wakes, Kiara awakens.' She opened her eyes. Her mind was working frantically, trying to figure out what was going on.

'Rise, traitor,' said the novices as one, and Kiara did.

The Great Mother sat on her dais, a distorted reflection of the woman who had bonded Huren to Kiara not six years previous. There were fifteen of her tribe sisters forming a circle around her. Huren was within the circle too but he was strapped securely to a table.

'Your loyalty to The Tribe has wavered and been severed, Kiara Tribeswoman. You can have only one master and that cannot be your heart. The Goddess has granted you the chance for redemption through sacrifice.' One of the sisters stepped forward and offered Kiara a hunting blade. 'To be redeemed you must kill your new master and be brought back to us or sacrifice your treacherous heart to the Goddess.' Kiara couldn't believe what she was hearing. She looked around for support from someone, anyone, but was met only with stony countenance. None of these women had shed a tear or even felt an emotion since their own redemptions.

'Remove and ingest the heart that keeps you prisoner and you will be free to re-enter the fold.' Kiara felt tears trickle down her cheeks. She looked at Huren, and he too was crying. 'I love you, My Heart,' was all she said as she picked up the knife.

Dogface or: How not to date a writer

BARBARA LOVETT

I find Humphrey, 35, poet, journalist and writer while my boss is out to lunch. His Matchnet profile says:

Do not try to lead lives but be lead by life. Do not struggle for answers but enjoy the questions! We rarely get what we want in the way we want it at the time we want it. What we get is what we need and require to further our evolvement unconsciously and emotionally, even if we miss this, deny it or fight against it. I therefore try not to baulk against confusion but let my path be dictated quietly. Either it takes me to a better place, the river that underlines my life or I struggle and cope as it happens. I know I sound absurdly spiritual and mellow-yellow but this is what I have salvaged from the fire.

His picture shows thick, dark hair and a lean face partly concealed by his raised arm, his middle finger pointing upwards to whoever took the photograph.

'Why are you giving me the finger?' is my chat up line.

'Because I like to put it in careful places,' his immediate reply.

'Carefully I hope,' is my response, which catapults me into my very first cybersex session.

I gently open his belt and unbutton his shirt.

He rips off my clothes.

I tenderly pull down his trousers.

He pushes me into the office toilet cubicle with pure male force.

I touch his cheeks and wipe away a stray eyelash.

He sucks my breasts until I scream.

I lovingly spread my legs.

He fucks me with my face against the wall.

He types faster than I and still manages to spell more words correctly.

I leave work early and go shopping for stockings and lacy underwear.

When I get home I find this in my inbox:

Hey Pink!

Do not worry that I am one of the sick creatures hell bent on using this peculiar medium as a means of procuring their own needs without ever making it a convergence of mutual desires! I do not fall into the category of the sexual terrorist or predator. I merely wish to seduce you with my combined wit, charm, intelligence, seductive eyes and the extensions that I am proud of. I long to immerse myself into your highways and byways of language and logic, emotion and sentiment, engender further brightness of spirit and begin an absorbing intersection of selves.

I hope this protracted piece of meandering nonsense seeps and slinks though your bloodstream, wends its way from page to eyes and infiltrates every little nerve, cell, pore and fibre so that the words find purchase in your inner self. Along with the depth of sentiment and sincerity that surely flows through them!

Humphrey

On the phone he quotes Shakespeare and Freud and promises to analyse my dreams and show me his collection of fountain pens. He interviews movie stars for newspapers and magazines and has a bizarre story about every single one of them. His voice is low and each sentence is an innuendo or a play on words. He has an endless number of names for my intimate body parts and meticulously describes the various aggregate states of his super-hard hard-on, a lush well of semen he successfully wanks up to six times an hour. Whenever I wonder if he is a freak, he distracts me with a joke. I giggle so much I don't mind I hardly get a word in.

The night he wants to meet I have a ticket for the National Theatre. As always with Shakespeare, the dialogue might as well be spoken under water and by the time I start to understand a word all characters are dead.

The interval I spend in the ladies' toilet, piling on make-up, squeezing into a short skirt and low cut top.

'Meet me at Cleopatra's Needle,' he texts. 'I'm in a brown corduroy suit.'

Brown Corduroy? I almost change back into my old, sweaty sweater.

He's going to explain Shakespeare to me, I remind myself. He's going to analyse my dreams and tell me more about the movie stars.

While I walk across Hungerford Bridge he calls.

'I'm in my car in a side street. Lift your hand when you reach the phallic Needle.'

I like the thought of him watching me walk through the night as I follow his voice into a side road, ready for an adventure and maybe more, oh hopefully so much more.

'I'm right here in the car,' he whispers in my ear. 'I'm getting out. Here I am.'

The door of a puny red Fiat opens, and a matchstick man dressed in puke brown steps out.

He bows and scrapes and looks at me expectantly.

I struggle to pick up my face from the floor.

This is the ugliest man I've ever seen in my life.

And we're not talking plain ugly here. We're talking children screaming, milk souring, police marching in with facemasks ugly.

His head is a bald greyhound snout. It consists of a long nose, paper-thin lips and watery pinhead eyes filled with apologetic devotion.

Shakespeare, Freud, pen-collection, movie stars, my soul mate, are the thoughts I cling to while I shake his moist spider hand.

The second we sit in the pub he reaches underneath my skirt. I find it easier to leave his fingers where they do no harm than push him away. We talk Anaïs Nin, Philip Roth and Woody Allen. He shows me his golden fountain pen and I show him my pink and purple ones. He promises to make me a tape of his favourite songs while underneath the table his fingers stumble through nowhere land.

Back on the street the big, wet tongue behind his razor sharp lips plants watery kisses on my face in a surprise attack.

I lose my balance and we almost both fall over. He drags me into a dark doorway, where he continues to slobber over me.

I stop him and look into his milky blue eyes trying to find something attractive in them.

He watches me with panting anticipation.

I rest my head on his shoulder and let him hold me, because holding on to someone is what I've been missing most. My nose picks up his smell, the smell of old soap that sits in folds of dirty skin and never gets rinsed off by a hot shower. I back away.

'If you only want to talk, that's ok,' he says.

We walk back to his car.

'What do YOU want?' I ask once we sit inside.

He is too busy to reply.

Shakespeare, Freud, dreams, pens - my soul mate is arching his back over his fast moving hand, moaning like a horny monkey walking on hot coals.

On the bus home I receive twenty-three texts.

There are seven messages on my home phone.

The next morning he sends this e-mail:

Oh, Pink. Thanks for an evening that was a mixture of delights. Nowhere and never before have lips as soft or kisses as spirited been tasted. Your charms and your assets are grand. You have a delicacy and silken texture that must reflect the purity of your soul.

It is like the finest fur, the sweetest rose, the lightest feathers, the quintessence of beauty. To travel over your body, to run my lips and fingers around your smooth beyond smoothness skin is a joy to behold and beseech again and again.

Just this for now: I am not a here today gone tomorrow fly by night feckless and ferocious fucker. When I encounter someone whose outlook, sense of humour and energy, not to mention their other charms make me enthralled and delighted, then I resolve never to surrender their involvement in my life.

I touch you in all the places that move and still you. I move myself towards you and relish the day when your lips' pleasant music can be heard through mine, chiming merrily together.

Humphrey

I read his words again and again and again.

Shakespeare, Freud, movies, pens, dreams and a tape only for me.

Maybe we didn't lose our balance when he kissed me? Maybe it was the earth shaking?

I accept his invitation to dinner at Joe Allen's two days later.

We are supposed to meet at eight. At seven, seven fifteen, seven twenty, seven thirty, seven forty-four and seven fifty-two he texts to let me know he is already there.

He is as ugly as I remember, with the added attraction of a perfect purple pus pimple on top of his nose.

I learn all about the pain of growing up without a father, the confusion of having his surrogate parent neighbours lure him into their bed when he was fourteen and the strains of squeezing into two condoms to please his last girlfriend.

He frequently mentions an ex but I don't ask him to elaborate. Ex is ex, right?

Twice we get interrupted because his mobile rings. The words he uses are grades, teachers, time tables, homework and books— which reminds me:

'I googled your name but none of your articles came up.'

He shows me his business cards which say profession: 'writer' but admits that at the moment he works mostly as an English tutor.

His fingers slide underneath my skirt.

'We should take our profiles off Matchnet and make this relationship work,' he says.

At the table next to us a dozen gay men with pumped up bodies, perfectly groomed hair and stylish clothes laugh and chat while the Muppet next to me moves his dried prune head up and down and chews his food with an open mouthed grin.

Don't be stuck up on looks, I tell myself. Beauty is nothing.

Shakespeare, Freud, my dreams, he is going to make me a tape.

'Okay. Let's take our profiles off.'

I invite him to a performance of 'The Rape of Lucretia' at the Linbury Studio. He is wearing his brown corduroy suit and a green shirt. The spot on his nose has turned into a crater the size of Vesuvius. I pray I don't run into anybody I know. As soon as the lights go out his hands are underneath my skirt. He never once looks at the stage.

'This is our third date,' he says after the show and hands me a bottle of champagne.

We have lots in common, is still my mantra. His looks are God's punishment for my obsession with handsome men. I need to give him a chance.

Although I know the way home, he stops several times to check the map. He runs two red lights. Whenever he changes lanes somebody toots.

In my house, he pours the champagne. He takes one glass and knocks the other to the floor with his elbow.

'Leave it, leave it,' he grunts and kisses me and spits a mixture of stale champagne and acidic saliva into my mouth.

Then he makes me kneel down and pushes my upper body onto the coffee table.

It's an ideal position. I don't have to look at him, cannot smell him, and barely feel him. I close my eyes and pretend he's a man and not a caricature - until he tries to open my bra. His beetle fingers contort around the simple clipping mechanism - an unsolvable mystery to him.

I get up with a sigh and drag him into my bedroom to get this over with.

'Can you shut the windows?' he asks.

'Why?'

'Why, burglars of course.'

While I do him the favour I hear the soft hurried sounds of undressing behind my back.

I turn around and watch him take off his green shirt, a black undershirt, a gray vest, the brown trousers, two pairs of striped boxers, tight underpants and two pairs of socks.

All that is left when he has finished is a white skeleton, a heap of ramshackle bones with a nose and a hose.

'See, I'm not the most attractive man in the world,' he says.

No kidding.

'But if somebody asked me what my most beautiful body part was I would say my penis.'

He strokes it with a happy smile.

Don't be superficial, I tell myself. Don't be shallow. You've only slept with one man in your life before. You need to accept that not everybody is a six-foot former hockey player with a bum of steel. Keep your eyes closed. Don't breathe.

We fumble around under the sheets and I wish I was far, far away where people procreate by cell division.

He pokes his thingy against my tummy and it occurs to me that he never made me a tape, never showed me his pen collection, never read Shakespeare to me and the one dream I told him about he interpreted as a sign that a skinny, intelligent Jew will change my life.

'I forgot to bring condoms,' he mumbles. 'Do you mind if - '

I push him away.

'No way, you stupid - '

I can't finish the sentence.

His own hand is doing the job.

The extension he's proud of whizzes around like an out of control water hose. It sprays mashed potato sauce against my bedroom wall until it looks like a Pollock painting.

His mobile rings.

'My ex,' he says and disappears into my bathroom.

As he retreats I notice a big hairy mole on his back.

Is there really not one single bit on him that is not repulsive?

While I hear subdued mobile talk from outside I stare at the ceiling.

Does sex with a soul mate have to be like that? Wouldn't I be better off with a friendly rubber doll?

He returns.

'I think you should know -,' he says. 'I think you should know we sort of - my ex and I - erm - she is my wife and - we actually still live together.'

He pauses and studies my face but I have no energy to react.

I'm not shocked that he lied. I'm shocked that -

Somebody out there was willing to marry Dogface.

'We're separated of course. Totally separated.'

Quasimodo managed to get married.

'You know how it is in London. She doesn't have a place to stay.'

A woman promised to spend the rest of her days with Pus-nose.

'We're legally separated and in the process of getting a divorce. I don't want to lie to you, but it's a lengthy process.'

Who on earth? Who on earth? Who on earth said yes to this creepy creature?

'Anyway, she meets men on Matchnet all the time and now she's in love and it pisses me off.'

He got married to someone who is capable of finding somebody else.

'I thought you would appreciate me being honest.'

Dogface found a wife.

'I need to go.'

In the bathroom I find that he somehow managed to completely unroll the toilet paper, drop the soap in the bin and dunk the towel into the toilet.

I shower until the hot water runs out, put the sheets in the washing machine with a triple load of detergent and disinfect kitchen and bath.

The sperm on the wall washes off without leaving a trace.

I cry with relief.

The next morning:

Pink: Let me be brief! I want to condense rather than put this into a flabby, flatulent and florid piece of prose. I had begun our dialogue with one intention only. I was impressed with your mind and impressed with your cultured antennae. The more I knew, the more I wanted to know. When we met I wanted to fuck you but you pushed me back and craved tenderness instead. Your searchlight eyes gave you away. The wish for a hug suggested the depth that our erotic encounter sidestepped. I wonder if you are assuming a romantic bridge is being created. The clues in your demeanour suggest that it is romance and depth you search. I like you enormously and fancy you, but I want nothing but fucking with dialogues. If you are happy with this, let me know. The sooner the better!

Humphrey

After a week of silence he giggles onto my answer phone that while we both took off our Matchnet profiles he remained on J-Date, where he met this wonderful French girl he has deep and precious feelings for.

'I think it would be healthy for both of us to meet again,' he says. 'I would love to stay good friends with you.'

He sends so many e-mails my laptop clogs up and he calls so many times my mobile breaks down.

I feel sorry for him.

Maybe as friends we will be able to read Shakespeare and Freud and my dreams?

He cancels our first date as friends because he is flying to Cologne to see a nineteen-year-old German girl he fell madly in love with online.

He cancels our second date because he is taking his wife out for dinner to discuss plans of possibly getting back together.

He cancels our third date because the new love of his life is flying in from Rome.

I cancel our fourth date because I admit to myself that I positively loathe the rat.

'I understand that you're jealous,' he whimpers on my answer machine. 'You're jealous because I never loved you and now found true love with that woman from Liverpool but I
really - '

The answer machine shatters into a hundred plastic pieces as it hits the wall.

There is no formal seating for 'Power Struggle'

DANIEL MAITLAND

There is no formal seating for 'Power Struggle.'
Sit where you like,
and for God's sake
strap yourself in;
while greasy public schoolboys
and bitter, decaying ex-miners
plant their heels
and hold on with 'burning' hands
to the faux lightning
and meaningless babble
of 'Office'

Skyros Centre - Hill to the Sea

MARTI MIRKIN

Butterfly hillside
High
Diving hawks
spiralling down in loose formation

Dawn till dark

White horse on the hill, so still
So still.
Hibiscus descending,
a red scented waterfall,
White butterflies, red ones,
from flower to flower,

White horse on the hill,
My beauty,
So still
Alone on the hillside
In sunlight and tethered
Alone in the tall grass
the flowers around you.

Sea birds ride the wind
Rising hot from the meadow
their shadows
a pattern
on the hillside below
Their shrill cries
Songs of freedom
crisscrossed and free
On their run to the sea.

A Sense of Loss

MARK KIELY

We were both there. Sitting in a large, modern church. The walls were whitewashed, the pews made of soft, polished wood. The ceiling was low and flat with rows of fluorescent lights. We sat side-by-side, the aisles so full that we were pressed against each other.

To my left a woman was crying, a sodden mass of tissue in the hand that dabbed at her eyes. There had been a terrible tragedy, and we all understood the sense of loss, the sense of grim bafflement that filled this place. I wanted to speak to you, but words seemed inappropriate. Nevertheless, some of our fellow mourners were talking amongst themselves, and a low hum of conversation could be heard beneath the sporadic wail of despair.

At the front of the church, a six-foot statue of Christ hung upon the wall, the loin-clothed figure fixed upon a cross. The altar stood deserted. Where was the priest? These people had come here for comfort, for healing. This was how we intended to make sense of past events and to comprehend our pain. Yet the priest had deserted us. Surely this was some kind of betrayal.

My eyes were fixed upon you when the sound of the first, un-comprehending gasp reached us. You were looking straight ahead, and the transformation in your expression was so startling that a sense of dread slithered along the length of my spine and wrapped itself around my throat. I looked around just in time to see the fig-ure leap down from its perch onto the top of the altar. Knees bent and body hunched forward, with difficulty its head turned from side-to-side, examining its surroundings. Then, with two feet, Christ launched himself forward to stand at the front of the packed aisles.

My first reaction, one of disbelief and confusion, was supplanted by an emotion so deep and so pervasive that it very slowly came to encompass my entire consciousness. Beyond fear, beyond reverence, beyond awe. It was an overwhelming doubt, a sudden awareness of the insubstantiability of everything I had ever known. Faced by this figure of Christ, all meaning seemed to fade. This destruction of my sense of reality was so profound that I felt a longing to retreat, to cling to my past, to hide amongst its hollow untruths.

There was panic and movement about me. You were remarkably calm, sat unmoving upon the bench while those around us screamed and hugged and fled. Holding your hand within mine, I rose to my feet and looked all around at this scene of mayhem. As you suddenly pulled free your hand, I looked back towards the front of the church. All understanding of myself drained out of my body as I found its eyes fixed upon me. Hand outstretched and finger pointing in my direction, with unsteady, fitful steps, it was walking down the aisle.

You remained motionless, and, unable to pass by the people to my left, I found myself scrambling over the tops of the pews in my attempt to flee. Turning once, as I managed to leap out into the aisle, I saw that it had passed you and that the eyes were still fixed upon me. For a brief moment, I attempted to meet the eternal stare of those expressionless wooden eyes, but terror bade me to turn away.

The people blocking my escape began to move away from me. Scurrying back to their hiding-places behind the pews, this enabled me to run towards the doors at the back of the church. I could hear the slapping of its feet upon the floorboards as it pursued me.

At the rear of the church, a short corridor curled round to the left, past the notice board and the holy water. At the end of this corridor, the doors that should be propped open during a service were closed. I threw them open and almost fell outside.

The doors swung shut, and I was alone out here. Any of the con-
gregation who had fled ahead of me had carried on their flight. The
rest, perhaps, had become placated by its fixation on me. I had
made no move, was still standing beside the doors. Fear and curiosity battling for supremacy, as they so often will, I hesitantly
reached a hand back. Gently pushing the doors open a crack, there
was no sound at all. Opening them further, I peered inside. The corridor I had fled down was empty. That thing seemed to have
stopped in its pursuit of me.

Letting go of the door, I took a few steps backwards away from
the church. It was an unspectacular day, a day without a season.
Neither sunshine nor rain filled the sky. There were colourless
clouds above. Spinning round, I watched as a double-decker bus
passed by. As if they had not been there before, my surroundings
grew in my consciousness. It was a high street, just like any other.
There were people - men, women, carrying shopping, carrying
children, smoking, talking - and they knew nothing of the sights I
had just seen.

A narrow strip of short grass surrounded the church and then no
fence, no gate. The architecture, like the modern interior without
altar rail or lectern, was egalitarian and welcoming. I stood with one
foot on the grass and the other on a concrete paving stone as strangers passed me by. From across the street, the smell of sweet and
greasy food escaped a bakers. It was lunchtime, and a long queue
stood at the counter. Our daily bread.

This surely was real. Lunchtimes and buses and people and... a
loud vibrating noise, the ground shaking slightly, something above
me... a railway bridge seemed to appear overhead with a commuter
train hurtling across it. A couple of faces peered down at me. So
much life, so much energy. Like a Monday morning. I loved Monday mornings. Yes, this was real. I was close to where I lived, I
knew that now, and if I stood here long enough, a friend's face
would appear among those passing me. We could go for coffee and
talk about our pasts, our futures, how we felt today. We could share
stories about people we knew, but the one person we would not talk
about was you.

For you were still inside that place from which I had fled. And not only you - so was that thing that had terrified me, a thing less than God but born of eternal uncertainties. I could walk away from here and the fear I had felt. I could immerse myself in this day. I could celebrate the excitement and the joy of existence, like jumping off the diving board and swimming in life. Or I could return to you and the mysteries that had taken their form in that statue.

The choice was mine.

Hard hats to be worn at all times

JOANNA CZECHOWSKA

Here I lie - freshly washed, carefully made up, smartly dressed and dead. I can see myself quite clearly from my vantage point on the ceiling.

They have put me in the brown suit, complete with waistcoat that I last wore for my boss's wedding. This will be its first funeral. There's a white handkerchief in my top pocket and expensive gold cuff links at my wrists. My head is propped up on a little red pillow. The undertaker has carefully painted rouged cheeks, lipstick and acres of beige foundation on my face. He has almost managed to conceal the black circles under my eyes and the purple bruises on my cheek, the gash on my nose. My feet have been squeezed into the black lace-up shoes I never wore because they were too small. The pale-wood coffin, however, fits precisely with a half-inch to spare all round. The lid is lined with an expensive-looking dark red satin. I should make the most of the time before they close me up. I'll be a long time staring at that lid.

A woman and a little girl are standing in the room. The little girl looks at me and then up at her mummy. 'What will we do without his money?' she asks.

The woman shrugs and smiles her old smile. 'Don't worry, pet-al,' she whispers.

The woman is Liz, I can see her now. I can see every pore on her skin, every tiny line on her forehead, each separate black eyelash.

She is looking older - far older than her years. There are deep shadows under her eyes, her jaw line is sagging and her mousy blonde hair is a frizz of ill discipline. Even her clothes are baggy, shabby and ill considered.

How she has changed. I remember her at 17, wearing her Park Road School uniform, her hair in a neat little clip and her nose in a book. She would actually stroll along the street reading. She walked past me every day on her way back home. Most of the other lads on the building site would call and whistle.

'Hello, darling. Give us a smile.'

I never called out, it's not dignified. The others would yell at anything in a skirt. Then one day she walked past with a carefree air, swinging her bag.

'Where's your book?' the lads yelled. She turned and looked at me. I doffed my hard hat and smiled. She smiled back - a glorious, everlasting smile - and I knew, I just sensed that she was destined to be mine. Completely and eternally.

I'd never had anything that was mine. Abbey Street is a well-known slum area of town, and our tiny terraced house held a total of eleven brothers and sisters. Everything was communal, borrowed, hand-me-down, charity shop - the beds, the clothes, the shoes, the comb.

But Liz wasn't second-hand. She was brand, spanking new, never been used, totally fresh. Strangely, she liked me. She came into the little corner café where I was having tea and a bacon sandwich. My hands were filthy with cement dust, my jacket and trousers grimy and my work boots were caked in dried mud.

'Hello, book girl. Can I buy you a cup of tea? My name's Len,' I said.

Liz lived in Allestree, where the houses had gaps in between, cars parked in the drive and trees down the street. She was an only child and she had her own private bedroom, her own personal clothes and her own comb. Her parents never shouted or threw things.

I bought her a cup of tea and a bag of chips. She seemed interested in me, in my life, in my family.

'Tell me about your brothers and sisters, Len,' she said.

I told her about Mike who talked to his pigeon all day, about Marcie who worked in the launderette, about Jack who was doing eight months inside for burglary and little Pat who was epileptic and autistic and just sat in a corner, rocking.

'You're lucky. I wish I had brothers and sisters,' she said. 'I wish my house had noise, talk, rows. I want passion, excitement, anger, jealousy - anything.'

'I can give you all that,' I said.

We ran away. We just left one day.

Liz packed a small bag of clothes and her teddy bear. She left a brief note for her parents on the kitchen table. I took my week's wages and the clothes I stood up in. We caught the bus to Nottingham.

In a post office window we found an advert for a flat. It turned out to be a tiny place, with green, speckled wallpaper and fifties furniture. There was one gas ring and we had to share the bathroom. It was damp, cheap and nasty but we took it.

We were lucky because there was plenty of work around for men like me. They always needed brickies, hod carriers, plasterers - men with plenty of brawn who didn't think too much. I started work immediately.

But it was just a few days later that I came home and Liz dropped her bombshell. She just stood there and said it like it was a perfectly normal thing to say. I couldn't believe it. It was a knife-twisting stab to the stomach.

'I've got a job,' she said smiling all over her pretty, stupid face.

I stared at her.

'What?' I yelled.

'Shush - I just said I've got a job. It's at the little greengrocer on the corner and I start...'

She never saw my punch coming. It landed right on her jaw and sent her hurtling on to the back wall. She sat there holding her cheek, staring at me in absolute astonishment. It's funny, my mum never had that expression on her face when Dad hit her - she always had a look of defeated resignation.

'You have not got a fucking job,' I bellowed. 'If you want a job, it's here. Your job is to wait here until I come home. Your job is to be here for me.'

She stayed where she had fallen all night, crying softly and clutching her little teddy bear. In the morning, she stood up and made some bacon and eggs for my breakfast. I took a £10 note out of my pocket and put it on the table.'

'It's a huge multiplex cinema we're building,' I said. 'We cleared away streets of slums. It's going to be a massive project so there'll be work for years. No need to worry about money at all, is there?'

Liz said nothing. I kissed her on the cheek and went out.

One Friday night, I went out for a drink with the lads. We started out in the Prince of Wales just next to the site and moved onto the Feathers, the Crown and Greyhound and then the Rose.

I got back to the flat at two a.m. and stood swaying in the little room. Liz was lying asleep on the sofa, her huge pregnant body cradled round her teddy. I looked around the place and that's when I saw it. I'm always on the look out for clues and this time I'd caught her red-handed. On the little table - there was not one but two tea mugs. There was also a plate with a few biscuit crumbs on it. She'd had someone in here.

I howled with rage, grabbed her cardigan and dragged her off the sofa. Her large soft body fell with a thud on the floor.

'Who is he?' I screamed, kicking her in the back. 'Who have you had in here? Whose baby is that in your belly?'

She pushed back her hair and clutched at my leg.

'It's your baby, Len, it's yours.' Tears ran down her face and her nose was snotty. 'It was only Margaret from downstairs who came in for a cuppa. Don't be angry, Len. She only stayed about ten minutes.'

'I WILL NOT HAVE STRANGERS IN MY FLAT,' I said, kicking her with each word.

She crawled around on the floor trying to reach for her teddy. I grabbed it and hurled it out of the window as far as I could.

Liz had a baby girl - she called her Gina. She was a crumpled, red little thing with a face like an angry fist.

At the hospital, the nurse wrapped her in a thin, white blanket. 'Do you want to hold your daughter, Mr O'Connor?' she said.

'No,' I said, 'that stuff's for women.' Liz was lying silently in the bed, looking up at the ceiling. The baby was lying in the crib next to her bed.

'Your wife will need extra care and attention,' whispered the nurse. 'The health visitor will call to check up on her when you get home. It's very important that she doesn't feel isolated and sad as that can lead to post-natal depression. That's serious and should never be ignored.'

I brought Liz back to another flat I'd found while she was in hospital. Health visitors! I didn't want nosy old women poking around my home and my wife - not that strictly speaking we were actually married in the formal sense.

Being one of the more experienced lads at work, I was given extra responsibilities. And because there was so much work, they were always bringing in casual labour. Once they had this kid come on site - youth work experience they called it. He was about sixteen, and as green and callow as they come. He didn't have proper work clothes or gloves or boots. No one had even given him a hard hat. He'd only been there a couple of hours and was pushing a wheelbarrow full of bricks. He bent down to lower it to the ground and stood up straight. I turned round just in time to see the steel girder hanging from the crane swing about and take his head clean off. It just snapped off and rolled into a trench. You get a lot of accidents on building sites. We never even knew his name.

Liz came up to the site one day with Gina in the pushchair. She brought my sandwiches because I'd left them on the kitchen table.

We had a new site manager, Mr Craven, and when he said something, even if it was serious, he always followed it with a little laugh. I saw Liz walk up to him.

'Is Len around?' she said.

'You must be Mrs O'Connor,' he said. 'Your husband's over there. Ah, you've brought his lunch. Now there's a kind lass. Hey, what happened to your eye? That's a real shiner,' and he laughed.

'It's nothing,' said Liz. 'Sometimes little Gina here hits me with her head by mistake. She doesn't mean to.'

'Hey, Len. Your missus is here,' said Mr Craven. 'She says your little girl beats her up.' He chortled loudly.

I looked coldly at Liz. 'Hello, love. Thanks for these.'

Mr Craven was watching us. As Liz was leaving, he went over and talked to her. I strained to hear what they were saying but I couldn't. Liz looked frightened, glanced in my direction, shook her head and hurried away. Mr Craven walked up to me, laughed and wandered off.

I gave Liz a good thrashing that night, I can tell you. Next day she lost the baby she was carrying. But I'm sorry to say she deserved it. She only had herself to blame.

Mr Craven was talking about starting his own construction business. He wanted me to join him. He told me the pay would be better if I came in with him and I'd have more control over what I did. He said I wouldn't be just a small cog in a big machine; I'd be someone special, someone of note.

This is good. Mr Craven wants me, he admires my work. He certainly takes a great deal of interest in me. He even invited Liz and me to his wedding. He was getting hitched to some old bird - second time round for both of them.

We sat there at the reception in an old church hall. Mr Craven fussed over Liz, getting her drinks and asking if the food was to her liking. A strand of hair kept falling over her face. I raised my hand to brush it away and Liz leapt back in her chair nearly falling over backwards. I saw Mr Craven look at her and laugh. He was probably comparing her to the old mutton dressed as scrag-end he'd just married. Look at that woman - fat, fifty and wearing a tight purple suit while my Liz is pretty, slim and wearing a pale yellow dress.

Then I realised I'd never seen it before. Where had she got that dress? When she went out to the toilet, I followed her to the lobby. I grabbed her arm.

'Who gave you that dress?' I hissed.

'I bought it. I had some money in an old post office account. Don't you like it, Len?'

I gripped her arm as tight as I could and she winced. I was just about to speak when I saw Mr Craven in the doorway.

'Liz,' he called. 'Come on in and have a drink.' I quickly let go of her arm and she hurried back. Mr Craven smiled at her as she passed and laughed. Then, oddly, he shot me a look of pure malice. I couldn't work it out. He didn't speak to me during the rest of the evening. What on earth is going on? Never mind, it's work tomorrow. I'll talk to him then.

But here I am wearing that brown suit again. Only its second outing. You get lots of accidents on building sites.

Our Street

EMILY WIFFEN

*This is the first chapter of a novel, **Our Street**, which follows eleven year old Isla in her mission to uncover sinister goings on in her outwardly respectable South London street.*

People say that nothing happens in our street. People are wrong. The problem is that people don't look. Or maybe they look but they don't see. Or maybe they see but they don't notice. I don't know. But I look and I see and I notice.

It's always been that way. It was me who saw that Mrs Elliot was wearing the same dress as she wore to last year's Christmas party and it still didn't fit her. It was me who looked at the washing and saw that it'd been outside Number 18 for two days and asked if anyone had checked on Mr Everson recently. He'd died. It was me who noticed that there was a lot less whiskey in the bottle at Father Maguire's than there had been last week. I noticed all these things.

I used to tell people what I saw but they told me not to be nosy so I stopped telling them. I have tried my best to stop looking but I can't help myself noticing. So I still notice and I still remember. Even when no one listens to me.

It helps that it's easy to notice things from our house. We live on a hill. Other people are always complaining about it.

'There are hardly any hills in London. Why do we have to live on one?' they say.

They complain that they have to drag their shopping up or down, walk up or down to the school, walk up or down to the train station. I like the hill. It means I can see lots of things. From my window I can see into the street in front of our house. I can see which cars stop where, who goes in and out of the houses, when the lights go on and off. Before people close the curtains at night I see all sorts. Our house is on the corner so from my room I can see the traffic, the waiting, the deliveries on the main road.

When I do leave my room, I can see from our hall and bathroom window into our back garden. Decking, lawn, swings, shed. Not that exciting but I can see into the other gardens in the street as well and over the fence into the street behind. There's much more to see down there. A patchwork of other people's secrets.

So I saw and I looked and I noticed it all. And I remembered it.

And I can tell you this much. A lot happens in our street.

One day I said to my Mother, 'Why does Billy Flanagan have all those bruises on his arm?'

'Be quiet, Isla,' she said.

We were in the queue in the Post Office on the hill, up the road from our street. Mrs Flanagan, with Billy on red reins, had been two people in front of us in the queue. There was always a queue. Mrs Allen, who was a pensioner and therefore cared a lot about Post Offices, said it was because they had closed the Post Office down the road and everyone had to walk up the hill to post their parcels and do bank things and collect their pensions.

Billy had bruises all up his arm. Little bruises, the size of coins. He was crying. Every time I saw Billy he was crying about something but I know that little kids cry about all sorts of things.

Billy's mum had straggly hair and always looked tired. My mother said this was because Billy's dad had walked out on her when Billy was small and it was hard for her to look after him by herself. Mother said we were lucky to still have my Father, even if he was always so busy. Billy lived in one of the houses at the bottom of the street by the school that had been turned into flats. His mum had a man living with her. He wore jeans that had white stains on them as he worked as a plasterer. Mother told me this in the same tone of voice that she used when she talked about graffiti on the bus stop and queues in the Post Office. He had straggly hair too. I'd noticed that Billy's bruises and crying had started about the time that the man came to live with Billy's mum. I told Mother this.

'Isla. Stop,' she said. 'Nosiness is not an attractive quality.'

I decided then that I would try to stop noticing things. I would definitely stop telling other people about what I saw. And I was worried about doing things that were not attractive.

Right now I go to a little school five minutes up the hill from our street. I've been going there since I was four and people there understood that I didn't always think the same things as everyone else. But next year, when I am twelve, I will go to the school at the end of our street and there are a lot more people there. My mother and my teachers whisper about whether I will 'fit in'. I knew then that to fit in I had to try to not do anything other people considered unusual or unattractive.

It seemed that thinking about Billy Flanagan was considered unusual and unattractive so I tried to stop. He'd started going to the nursery next to my school so I sometimes saw him across the playground. His bruises were getting worse and he was thin and scared looking. I wanted to talk to him but I knew Mother would be cross if I did. Still, I was worried but I told my mother and she didn't want to know. I couldn't do any more.

When they took Billy away, everyone in the street was shocked. The man who lived with Billy's mum had been hitting him for ages, according to their neighbour, old Miss Talbot, talking to Mother in a whisper when they met in the street. Social services had taken Billy into care. His mother was distraught, but she hadn't done anything to stop the man. She invited him into their house so she was as responsible as he was.

'How did none of us notice?' said Miss Talbot, shaking her head. My mother flashed a glance at me.

'I don't know,' said my mother.

'Little boys are always falling over and hurting themselves,' said Miss Talbot. 'How was anyone to know?' Mother looked at me again.

'There was nothing we could have done,' she said and that made me angry.

Maybe there wasn't much I could have done. I was eleven years old. I didn't want to make my mother cross. I didn't want to be un-attractive. Who would listen to me if I said my own mother dismissed me without thinking? They were grown-ups. They could have talked to Billy or talked to his mother or the police. There was plenty they could have done about it. They just chose not to see, not to notice things. Why did they do that, I wondered? It seemed to me that they deliberately didn't notice what was right under their noses. Why was this? Why did they just let bad things happen right in front of them, like Billy being hit or Mr Everson being dead? It wasn't right.

It was then that I made my decision. This was my street. If bad things were happening then I should do something about them. Fitting in was less important than bad things like Billy getting taken into care. People like Jesus were forever pointing out bad things that were happening and getting into trouble about it. Father Maguire said in his sermons that we were supposed to be like Jesus. So if bad things were happening I should be like Jesus and tell people about them and make them stop, whatever other people said. But how would I make people believe me? I couldn't really help people like Billy if no one believed me. People hadn't even always believed Jesus, and he was God.

But I knew from school and the television that if you have evidence people have to believe you, because you have proof, and proof is important. If I'd had photos of Billy's bruises or a recording of him saying what happened then everyone would have had to believe me. I had to write everything down, keep a notebook, watch movements and times and make observations. There were three particular things I had to do. I had to notice things, then I had to collect evidence, then, once I had proof, I had to tell someone who would believe me. It wasn't going to be easy but I had to try. I was sure there were other Billy Flanagans out there and I couldn't just sit by and let what had happened to Billy happen to them.

The Aftermath

BARUCH SOLOMON

Colin's mother didn't approve of thunderstorms. They made her Colin fidgety for one thing, and when he was restless he tried to meddle with his manhood.

Miss Trimble was suffering in the heat. 'I do hope this weather breaks soon,' she was saying. 'I mean, surely it can't go on like this for much longer?'

She'd been knitting a shapeless cardigan for Colin and every couple of minutes she put her work down to fan herself with her magazine.

'Ah, but you don't know that, Hettie,' Colin's mother admonished, a little more vehemently than necessary. 'How do you know it won't go on for weeks? And then the weather may not break at all, but just cool down of its own accord.'

Colin, his mother and Miss Trimble were sitting outside their house on straight-backed kitchen chairs. The sun, a merciless white disc in a hazy sky, bore down on them relentlessly and the humidity was overpowering. Their yard was concreted over and everything, even the dandelions that grew through the cracks, looked parched or dusty. The only signs of vigour came from the freshly watered geraniums and petunias growing in tubs and hanging baskets.

'The thing about thunderstorms,' continued Colin's mother 'is that once one starts, you never know what it will lead to.'

She was sitting bolt upright with her arms folded. She didn't believe in giving in to the weather, but she'd allowed herself the indulgence of undoing a couple of buttons on her blouse. It was just possible to see the cleft in her bosom rising and falling as she panted for breath.

Colin was wearing his Sunday suit. He had a sort of faded respectability about him, so that he might have been taken for a lawyers' clerk or an unsuccessful insurance salesman. His crisp white shirt sported a large gravy stain and quite a few flies were attracted to something sticky on the front of his waistcoat; testimony to the meatballs and jam roly-poly he'd consumed earlier in vast quantities. His trousers were a little dirty at the knees and a pair of braces held them in place around his paunch as he rocked backwards and forwards on his chair, making low guttural noises.

Colin was bored and restless, He'd been happy enough for a while, kneeling on the ground with one of Miss Trimble's knitting needles and trying to stab the ants that swarmed everywhere. But his mother didn't like him playing with insects or tickling his chin with dandelion leaves. Anything that came up through the concrete made her feel uneasy.

'You ought to have the cracks filled in, Gertrude,' suggested Miss Trimble. 'Why don't you ask Mr. Harvey who does jobs at the sheltered housing? He seems like a nice young man.'

'I know, Hettie' Colin's mother conceded. 'Only I keep thinking I'll wait until… until... Colin!' she screeched. 'Colin! Colin, How DARE you!'

Colin had his hands down the front of his trousers. He was wriggling about on his chair and grinning ecstatically.

'Colin, take your hands away from your manhood this instant!'

Almost purple with heat and rage, Colin's mother half-rose from her chair and raised her hand as if to strike him.

'Did you see that, Hettie?' she said in an angry undertone to Miss Trimble, who was suddenly very intent on her knitting. 'No self-restraint. Can't take my eyes off him for a second!'

'Well, I suppose he is a bit rude sometimes,' Miss Trimble conceded, 'but he must get awfully tense in this weather. Perhaps it relieves him a little.'

'Relieves him!' exclaimed Colin's mother. 'Relief my foot; you don't know what you're talking about! The whole trouble with you, Hettie, is that you don't know the first thing about men.'

Colin, meanwhile, had taken his hands out of his trousers and was rocking back and forth again, moaning piteously. He held his arms up in front of his face as if to ward off a blow.

'Weak-willed, just like his father.' Colin's mother muttered. 'Sidney had no self-control either,' she added, not without a touch of pride.

'Shall we go and freshen ourselves up, Colin?' Miss Trimble suggested brightly. She always used the pronoun 'we' when she spoke to Colin, especially when it had to do with his bodily functions.

Miss Trimble could be exasperating sometimes, Colin's mother thought, not that it was her fault. The problem with Hettie was that she'd never known what it was like to be with a man. Perhaps that was for the best really, if her Sidney was anything to go by.

'She was right about the concrete though,' Colin's mother thought as she glanced around the yard. 'We ought to have the cracks filled in.' If only it were safe to have the whole thing taken up and re-laid. But that was another thing Hettie would never understand.

Still, what would she have done without Miss Trimble to help her? Have to call some ghastly social worker probably, like that Guinevere or whatever her name was, who turned up when she stopped bringing Colin to the day centre.

Colin's mother had a job keeping her on the doorstep. She was one of those over-friendly types they call 'touchy feely' nowadays. She wore more bangles than a gipsy and her costume was like a heap of brightly coloured rags she'd picked up at a jumble sale. She thought the geraniums and petunias in the hanging baskets were 'simply awesome!'

'You know, I think Colin is really connecting with Ursula,' she was saying. 'There's this like, really wonderful energy between them?'

That was another habit people had these days; telling her something and making it sound like they were asking a question.

'If I know my Colin, he does quite enough connecting without any help from you or Ursula,' Colin's mother had snapped.

'But, Gertrude!' Guinevere protested, advancing a step forward. 'Don't you think it's like, really amazing that Colin and Ursula are exploring their sexuality together?'

'It's Mrs. Privet to you,' retorted Colin's mother, 'and do you think you could take your hand off my wrist? You're invading my personal body space.'

She'd seen Ursula once in the Post Office. Guinevere was helping her cash her benefits. Ursula was short and stumpy and wrinkled. She dribbled continuously, and her hands hung limply from her forearms, as if broken at the wrists. Colin spotted her first. He gave a high-pitched squeal and tried to barge through the tape barrier.

'I think it would be nice for Colin to have a little girlfriend' Miss Trimble said. She had a kind heart, and she liked to see romance blossom, even for those like Colin.

'Hettie, for God's sake! Oh, what's the use?' Colin's mother wrung her hands in exasperation. She made one last attempt.

'Take this thunderstorm you're so looking forward to. It might happen all wrong, with the lightning and no thunder, or it may pour with rain but be just as hot and sweaty afterwards, so that you'll need another storm as soon as the first one's finished. Then again, it might just go on and on getting worse and worse until power lines come crashing down and buildings get destroyed.'

'But, Gertrude,' remonstrated Miss Trimble, 'haven't you ever experienced a day like this, when the air is so close you can hardly breathe? Suddenly, there's a brilliant flash. Then, when the explosion comes, it thrills you to your bones. The rain comes down in sheets and runs down the windowpanes in rivulets, washing everything clean. Then, when you wake up the next morning, the air is crisp and everything feels so cool and fresh.'

Colin's mother stared down at the concrete for a long time. Presently, the lines around her mouth softened and there was the shadow of a smile.

'Colin was conceived in a thunderstorm,' she said, finally.

It was almost dark, and the rain pounded and splattered against the window. Colin, his mother and Miss Trimble were sitting on straight-backed chairs around the kitchen table, drinking tea. The milk had turned, and little white bits floated around inside their cups. The dishes in the sink bore the remains of the smoked mackerel they'd had for supper.

Another flash lit the sky, illuminating the yard and surrounding buildings for a fraction of a second.

Colin rocked backwards and forwards excitedly, emitting a high-pitched sound like a kettle boiling. Miss Trimble sat hunched over her cup conspiratorially, as if the three of them were having a glorious adventure together.

'So, what was it like then, being with a man I mean?' she asked Colin's mother, leaning forward.

A loud crack ripped the air apart. Colin's mother sat stiffly in her chair, but Miss Trimble gave herself up to the explosion, hugging herself and wriggling ecstatically as if she were standing naked under a scalding hot shower.

Colin's mother hesitated for a moment.

'Having carnal knowledge of my Sidney was the most wonderful, beautiful thing that ever happened to me,' she began, a little reluctantly. 'But don't get me wrong. It's not like you think it is, with flowers and tenderness and cuddles. Have you ever seen a manhood when it's been aroused? There's no word for it. It's ghastly; like some huge pallid insect. And you can't even begin to describe the smell. The nearest thing is one of those French cheeses you get from the supermarket that they wrap in greaseproof paper. And Sidney never was particular about cleaning under his foreskin.

I was disgusted, and disgusted at myself for wanting him. And yet looking back, I wouldn't have changed a single thing about it. Even if I'd known what I do now, I'd still have surrendered myself to him. Yes, even with all the horror and pain and guilt I've suffered.'

'But what about afterwards?' Miss Trimble cut in. 'That's the bit I like to think about; when you've both satisfied your passions and longing and you're snuggled up together under the blankets, content and peaceful, going to sleep in one another's arms.'

'But Hettie, that's what I'm trying to tell you. Men never are satisfied. Allow a man to enter you once and he has to do it again. They never stop!' She looked at the floor. 'In the end, I had to halt Sidney's advances the only way I knew how.'

The doorbell rang. 'Who could be out and about in this weather?' Hettie exclaimed. They'll catch their death of cold!'

It was Guinevere. Her hair was plastered to her face and she was soaked to the skin.

'Well?' asked Colin's mother, unsympathetically.

'Mrs Privet? Hello, I'm sorry to bother you, only Ursula's gone missing, and I just wanted to check if... if...'

'Well she isn't here,' Colin's mother snapped, folding her arms with a satisfied expression.

'Well, it was just that what with her and Colin…. you know.'

'No I don't know!' Colin's mother retorted. 'And I don't want to know. Perhaps if you watched your patients instead of matchmaking, they wouldn't run away quite so often.'

'That's the thing with these coloured nurses,' she confided smugly to Miss Trimble after slamming the door. 'They've got all those fancy qualifications and they let their people run off in the rain. Where would my Colin be if I didn't watch him like a... Colin? Colin! Where are you Colin; are you in your room? Colin, if you're meddling with your manhood you'd better watch out!'

When Colin's mother went upstairs Miss Trimble sat on her own nervously for a few moments, then she went to look for him in the front room. The big bay window had been lifted and there was a trail of muddy footprints leading to the front path.

Upstairs the shouting continued. 'Colin, where are you Colin? Are you hiding from me Colin? Are you meddling with your man- hood, Colin?'

Sometime later, neighbours heard someone talking into a two- way radio and were dimly aware of a blue flashing light. After sev- eral hours, Colin finally burst into the kitchen, dripping wet and covered in mud. It had stopped raining by then and the night was clear and starlit.

'Colin, where on earth have you been?' cried Miss Trimble. 'We've been so.'

'Ursheller!' croaked Colin, pointing to his trousers.
'Maahnhood!' Then he collapsed, sobbing into his mother's arms.
As the morning sun rose over a fresh, pale blue sky, Colin's mother cradled him, holding him close to her as they swayed gently together from side to side.

They were sitting, Colin, Colin's mother and Miss Trimble, on straight-backed chairs at the kitchen table, watching the portable black and white TV. It was late afternoon. As the day wore on, it had become steadily more humid, and the kitchen stank of yester- day's smoked mackerel. It looked darker outside with the light on, and the sky was an unhealthy mixture of dull grey and parchment.

'You see?' Colin's mother was saying without much enthu- siasm, 'No sooner has a thunderstorm cleared the air than it's just as bad as it was before.'

Miss Trimble wasn't really listening. She'd already dropped countless stitches and her hands were trembling.

Colin was tugging Miss Trimble's arm excitedly, trying to at- tract her attention. He'd had an exciting day. The police car had turned up again, and he'd got to watch it with Miss Trimble from behind the curtains in his bedroom. Colin's mother had been shout- ing something about a warrant.

'But Gertrude, if you explain it to the police, I'm sure they'll understand. I mean, it's not as if Colin can help himself.'

'What makes you so sure it was his fault?' Colin's mother snapped. 'We're always blaming the men, but it's us women who lead them on!'

Colin started rocking back and forth again, pointing at the TV and still tugging Miss Trimble's arm. 'Look! isha my howessse!' he screeched.

Then the TV camera panned the crowd that had gathered outside, shouting and waving banners. At their head, a big brawny woman was trying to break through the police barrier while several ragged children ran amok. A young fresh-faced constable was attempting to reason with her. He looked embarrassed and anxious to avoid a tussle. Colin's mother recognised the woman. She'd often seen her slapping her kids at the bus stop near the tower blocks.

'You ought ter be ashamed of yerself. Protecting a bleeding pervert!' she was shouting, shaking her fist at the camera while the crowd cheered. Then she grabbed hold of her youngest, who was greedily sucking at a baby-bottle full of something fizzy and bright pink.

'We're just mothers caring fer our kids' she implored, holding the toddler up to the camera and doing her best to look tender.

Colin's mother marched into the front room. 'Mrs Gasforth!' she announced, poking her head out of the bay window. 'I'm not in the habit of harbouring criminals. I assure you that if my son returns here, you'll be the first to know about it!'

'For God's sake, be careful Gertrude!' Miss Trimble pleaded. 'And we can't hide Colin forever. The police will come back and… and…'

'Everyone blames the men.' Colin's mother had a far-away look in her eyes. 'But men are just weak. They can't help themselves. It's us women who are the evil ones. Don't think I haven't seen you flutter your eyes at Mr. Harvey from the sheltered housing. We're not happy until we've got them under our spell, wanting us and desiring us all the time. We torture them till they can't take any more. Sidney gave me the best few moments of my life, and that should have been enough. But no, I had to keep titillating him with my sensuality.'

'Look, I'm sure they won't send Colin to prison,' Miss Trimble remonstrated. 'He'll probably be looked after in a mental home or something like that.'

'Colin isn't going to suffer in an institution. I've seen what goes on in there. He'll be sat in front of the television all day with nothing to do but meddle with his manhood and pine over Ursula.' Colin's mother seemed to be fumbling with something under the table. 'That was why I did what I did to my Sidney, so he wouldn't have to suffer any more.'

There was a shout from the street and the sound of breaking glass in the front room. 'Yes, that's why I did it in the end; I couldn't bear to see Sidney in so much pain. And I know deep down it's what he wanted. Why did he keep one otherwise? He couldn't kill a bird or rabbit to save his life. He said it was to protect me from thieves and intruders, but Sidney was my only intruder. I wasn't going to let him pine away because he wanted to enter me, and I won't let my Colin suffer neither.'

She looked out of the kitchen window into the yard.

'Yes, there's no sense in just patching over the cracks. When this business is over, I'll get a hammer drill and take up the concrete myself.'

More breaking glass. Colin's mother sat down and started fiddling again under the table.

'Hettie, hadn't you best go upstairs and have a lie down? And shut the door so you aren't disturbed.'

But Miss Trimble didn't understand.

'My goodness Gertrude, I couldn't possibly think of going to sleep now!'

A flash of light outside. It might have come from the railway line.

'Yes, that's it,' Colin's mother was saying as she fumbled with the safety catch. 'Have the whole lot taken up and concreted over. Make a fresh start.'

Only Colin heard the small click. Suddenly he started grappling with his mother and wailing hysterically.

'Let go of me, Colin! Stop being so weak; you'll ruin the whole thing!'

Miss Trimble stared down at her knees, counting out of habit as she strained to hear the thunderclap through Colin's screams.

Four... five... six... seven... eight... nine... ten... eleven...

'I don't like thunderstorms,' Colin's mother said quietly.

The Aftermath

Looking For Clues

SUE LANZON

'Since I discovered the unconscious, I find myself much more interesting.' **Sigmund Freud**

He sits opposite me. He's asked to be there, in my consulting room. He's paying for my time. Yet his legs are crossed, his arms are folded, his body slants away from me at a curiously uncomfortable-looking angle as if he's trying to make a break for the door with his shoulder. 'Why is he shielding his left side?' I wonder, shifting my own body to mirror his position.

She tells me something completely, horrifically, spine-chillingly awful about her personal life, and bursts out laughing. Has she noticed I'm not laughing with her? Should I mention it? Her bared teeth remind me of a chimpanzee in distress.

Instead of saying 'My children are driving me nuts,' he says 'My children are driving *you* nuts.' Is he referring to himself here as one of my children? Does he really want to say *I'm* driving *him* nuts? Would Sigmund find this funny?

Then there's the one who, in telling me her current problem, perfectly reflects some aspect of my own. She starts to talk and I know what she's going to say next, because I woke up dealing with the same thing and... she says it. I'm aware of struggling not to betray myself. It's a close call. She sees a flicker of my eyelids and some part of her recognizes I am in a state of empathy, of rapport, beyond the usual. She doesn't know she knows this. I concentrate very

165

carefully as I suspect she has something unspoken about her person which I need to recognize in some way. As I offer her a new perspective on her situation, which may help her to deal with it more effectively, I realise that I'm telling myself what to do.

Erroll, my next-door neighbour and a tough cookie, says to me,

'Have you ever thought about the fact that if you put a space between the "e" and the "r" of the word "therapist" it looks like "the rapist?" '

His wife, Marjorie, a goddess whose wisdom and beauty are renowned throughout South London and beyond, sneers knowingly at the dark circles under my eyes.

'Your adrenals are shot, darlin'. Too much time spent listenin' to other people's crap. It too excitin' for yo' ass.'

'So which is it?' I bleat, glancing down at the cup of dark, bitter liquid Marjorie has thrust into my hand. 'Certainly, it can be argued that the uneven power dynamic between therapist and patient will inevitably render the patient a victim on some level. However, as any homeopath will tell you, the existence of psychic vampires masquerading as unwell humans is an undisputed reality.'

'Just be quiet now and drink.' Marjorie says.

Later, whilst lying in a very hot bath wondering if my adrenals are enjoying the rest or being pushed further into meltdown by the temperature of the water, my thoughts return to the opposing forces which can infect a therapeutic relationship, and the constructs which shape its direction.

Since I discovered the unconscious I find myself to be much more aware of the delicacy of human communication. I endeavour to translate a language whose meaning is unknown whilst being *constantly* reminded, (I'd just like to take a moment here to thank all my teachers, patients, children, parents, lovers, friends, cats and my many, many fans who've made it possible for me to be lying in this bath today, being reminded), that my translation is, by its nature, a subjective one. The only way I can ensure that my skill as a healer is not corrupted by this is to anticipate synergy - the making of something greater than the sum of its parts.

I need to engage with the patient as an equal in our humanity; provide a safe space between us in which they can lay out the concerns that have driven them to come; note all the different nuances of communication happening simultaneously on the physical, mental, emotional and spiritual levels; put them into some kind of coherent pattern or shape; scan my conclusions for contamination from my own issues; scan myself for vampire bites; offer this new configuration back in a way that invites the patient to participate in their own healing process and gives them something constructive to take home; accept resistance or denial as useful information regarding the pace of change; reflect on what the patient in turn has given me in the way of new insight and knowledge and somewhere, in among all this, prescribe a remedy.

(You may wonder why it is that homeopaths always have to look things up in books. Well, guess what, we're not looking up anything at all. We're just playing for time. You think you've come for a little something for your eczema? Think again).

Hopefully, this dynamic interchange between us acts as a conduit for mutual growth. The tricky bit is allowing the unconscious forces expression whilst not getting caught up in my own interpretation. No wonder we call it practicing.

The bathwater is now the wrong side of tepid. I reach for a towel, hoping I've succeeded in forestalling burnout for another day. Burnout? Meltdown? All this heat-inspired imagery. Is my unconscious trying to tell me something? Has the bath scorched my linguistic faculties? What was in that drink Marjorie gave me, anyway? Why do I ask so many questions?

The phone rings. It's Erroll to say my cat's been pooing on his lawn again.

'How do you know it's not foxes?' I counter, paradoxically now sharp as a pin after my long soak.

'Because,' he says, 'I happen to know cat shit when I see it.'

A long line of question marks skid to a halt as I confront Erroll's grasp of certainty, so much more muscular than my own. Then, realising he's waiting for a reply and noticing I'm dripping bathwater into the receiver, I yawn somewhat over-dramatically.

'Can we investigate tomorrow in the daylight, please, Erroll? Things will be a lot clearer then,' I say, rather pleased at my own impromptu stab at being sure of something, even if all I'm sure of is that things are unclear right now. Sharp as a pin, eh?

'Why not?' he says. 'Come by for a Marjorie Special in the morning.'

I look at my indistinct reflection in the mirror. Somebody once said that those who have all the answers are probably asking the wrong questions. As I rehearse giving this news to Erroll, the foxes start their nightly mating ritual - a noise which has become part of our inner city lives and which makes me think more of pigs being slaughtered than foxes obeying a biological imperative - then I think again. Instead I'll tell him that the word "therapist" comes from the Greek *theraps*, one who escorted the coffin at a funeral and can be translated therefore as one who travels alongside or, stretching the allusion further, a neighbour.

The clues are not in the sound of things, nor how they look nor even how they feel. It's the spaces between the objects that make synergy possible.

No doubt he'll think of something coruscating in reply, which will make me laugh as we examine the shit together on the lawn.

Cornfield at Sunset

EMMA MACKINNON

When the world is split
by dark and light
You're halfway there.

Night hunters
Moon traced
Guided by the sun's last fire.
Moving towards your own place
as the world spins
and burns in space.

You boys
In fields of corn
soft-soled at dusk
Your footprints hold
the stars' cast husks.

The Etiquette of Stalking

LYNSAY MACKAY

Carly pressed her hands to the base of her spine and arched her body as best she could. The new office chairs left much to be desired. How on earth was anyone supposed to get any work done when all they could think about was an aching back?

Not for the first time she let out a frustrated sigh, but once again she followed her anger with no action. Complaining would bring unwanted attention and she was not yet so deluded that she believed she could talk her way out of her recent activity.

Carly was a stalker. She had not set out to become a stalker or really knew how she had ended up this way, but she was aware that was what she was. Try as she might, she just could not seem to stop.

Online social networking had been introduced to her by a colleague. 'You've got to join, Carly, everyone else has,' Susan had said to her. 'You should see our group, Slaves to BSC Management, it's well funny.'

She had dutifully joined, never liking to be left out and had instantly seen the potential in the numerous networking sites. Within a week she had profiles on all of them; but that had just been the beginning. Within a month she was creating fake profiles, alter egos who did all the things that Carly only fantasised about.

Vi, the exhibitionist who bedded men and women en masse, who danced all but naked in nightclubs and demanded attention whenever she walked into a room. 'Don't wait for him to make the first move darling,' she wrote to her young protégé, 'Just walk right up to that boy and show him what he's been missing, if he doesn't like it he's probably gay and you should move onto the next one.'

In Ronnie, she created a contemptuous beauty that was never scared of a fight and always got what she wanted, no matter the cost to others. 'Don't feel bad if she cries,' she told one of her friend's husbands. 'If it's important to you then she should understand.'

Her sculpted young gay man was a favourite. Jamie drew praise and comment from men of all ages regardless of the fact that she had made him only seventeen. 'If you're good enough to fuck then you're good enough to meet his friends,' she responded to one email. People told secrets to the beautiful, and Carly now found herself full to bursting with information she could not even have dreamed of.

There were rules of course! She never created anyone below sixteen nor offered responses to those who looked or claimed that age. She *never* arranged meetings, and stopped responding to any who insisted more than thrice - three strikes and out, that was her motto.

She never put up pictures of herself and had shut down all bar one of her original profiles. She still needed one of course, to mask what she really used the sites for.

The sound of someone walking in her direction caused her to shut down all of the incriminating windows on her computer. The instant messaging she had been doing with Raoul could easily be restarted at any time; such things often kept her entertained during a slow afternoon in the office.

Carly looked up at the unwelcome passerby and gave a smile to Janet, a colleague who often tried to talk her into after work drinks. 'Will you be joining us this evening?' Janet asked.

Carly sighed ruefully, 'I really can't tonight Janet, my Gran is ill, and the doctors don't think she'll see out the week.' She let her face fall, staring vacantly at the space between her keyboard and screen. This was how she had seen people react to grief on television and it seemed to satisfy her co-worker.

Janet nodded sympathetically. 'It's hard to watch those we love pass, but it is often for the best, there is no pain in the afterlife.' Her hands touched her heart before one of them landed on Carly's shoulder. 'God will keep and protect her until you can be reunited.' Janet's smile was full of warmth and compassion; it made Carly want to be sick.

Carly wanted to scream at the woman that only the ignorant had faith, but she knew her place.

'Thank you, Janet, your thoughts and prayers are welcome.' She gently clasped the hand that had been left on her shoulder and offered a tight-lipped smile. It was enough. Janet squeezed her hand in return and left the workstation without looking back. Carly was free to do as she pleased once again.

Online social networking had changed an entire generation's ability to stalk and Carly had definitely embraced it. No skulking in bushes to find out what your friends were really doing (not that she would ever have contemplated that of course), now you could simply choose one of your many characters and use them to ask. That had been the original intention; just to keep a couple of tabs on her nearest and dearest and the distanced nature of the internet seemed to remove the sleaze and stigma attached to such things, everyone was doing it, weren't they?

Fingers moved without thought and suddenly Carly was back into one of her many e-mail accounts. In this one she was a forty-five year-old married mother of four, unhappy with a husband who gave her less attention than his collection of beer mugs. The responses she received no longer surprised her and she replied to most of them automatically.

The young prince willing to whisk her away was not new; most of them were acne-ridden boys who had even less sense of themselves than they did of what a woman was.

The middle-aged man, trapped in the same scenario. Loveless marriages were so much more common than people expected them to be, she had quickly grown bored of such things. Men or women who remained in these shells of relationships were hardly worth the time.

And finally, the father figure. Daddy! The man who would take care of you forever, the man who would never do anything to hurt you and yet knew nothing about you, truly the man who she would want to be with, if only she could let her shield down and invite him in.

There was a surprise e-mail in this collection though. A young female, Angel, barely out of university, she had questions that perplexed Carly. Why would someone her age believe she had problems that Carly's persona could fix?

No, she had not sought to run from the relationship, it was not abusive in the regular understanding of abuse. Yes she had tried to rekindle the romance on more than one occasion, all conventional avenues had been pursued and Carly smiled as she typed that there were even a few unconventional avenues that she had attempted. They had been so unsuccessful that her husband had reacted with shock and disgust; but at least it was a reaction she wrote with a wistful tone.

Over the next few months, through instant messaging and email, Carly learned many things about Angel. Through following Angel's social networking page and those of her friends and family she learned more, and with the help of what information she was given, search engines bolstered her knowledge. People forget that information stored on the Internet is forever.

Carly was midway through an extended email to Angel when she heard someone approaching her desk. It was Friday afternoon and she had known this was coming from morning. She looked at the clock on her computer and was surprised to realise it was so late.

'Thank the good Lord it's Friday, eh Carly?' said the smiling face of Janet, reaching Carly's desk just as she closed the last window on her screen. Carly nodded agreement and smiled back. It had become a painful ritual for Carly. There were only so many ways a person could say no before it became rude and though in Carly's mind that line had long been crossed, Janet still persisted. 'You got plans again or you think you could manage a drink tonight?' and there it was, the question Carly had come to dread. All she wanted to do was finish her email and get home to wait for the reply but she couldn't tell Janet that.

'Sorry Janet, I've got a date tonight,' she lied effortlessly.

'Really?' asked Janet, a flash of something unfamiliar passing through her eyes. 'You didn't say anything on your status. Is it someone I know?'

'I don't think so, just someone I met at my print workshop last week.' Carly was meticulous about the lies she told now, there were so many to keep up with that she kept a small diary with them all recorded in her handbag. It wouldn't do for people to *think* her deceitful.

Janet grinned conspiratorially, 'And does the mystery man have a name?'

'Mark,' she said a little too abruptly. For some reason the question hadn't occurred to her and she'd had to think fast, Carly hated thinking fast. She started to pack up to draw attention away from the response. 'Got an hour to make myself presentable, so I'd better be going.' This was getting far too awkward for Carly's taste and she was ready to make a quick exit.

'Well, I'll walk to your car with you then, I was just leaving as well. Maybe I'll be able to pin you down to a definite night out, just us girls,' Janet said as she swung the large handbag Carly hadn't noticed up on to her shoulder.

'Aren't you waiting for the others?' Carly asked casually. She had never enjoyed Janet's company and always made efforts to avoid the woman, especially alone, Carly suspected it was the God talk that made her so uncomfortable in her presence.

'We all agreed to meet there so we could drop off cars and what not,' she replied, 'give us girls a chance to freshen up.'

Carly was out of excuses and so bowed to the inevitable. 'Let's get going then.'

Carly tried to walk quickly but Janet's constant inane chatter and lack of pace prevented anything more than a stroll. The car park for the building was in the basement and quite large, it was ten long minutes before Carly was in sight of her car and could bring to a conclusion the whole tedious experience. They said their goodbyes and Carly headed to her car.

Shae greeted her at the door when she got home.

'Hello, little one,' she cooed, giving the cat a scratch behind the ear. 'Catch any mice for me today?' Carly took off her jacket and hung it up behind the door. There were a few letters on the floor and she picked them up then discarded them when she realised they were all bills or junk.

She entered her living room and flopped onto the couch. Her body went cold when her eyes fell upon the book sitting propped up on her TV. Her hands grasped for her bag, where the leather bound diary of lies should have been, but of course it wasn't there, it was on top of her television with a small note attached to it.

Shaking violently she somehow managed to cross the floor and pick up the note. It fell from numb fingers; three little words seared her vision.

Who's watching you?

For the Sake of Daniel

ANAND NAIR

Daniel put his latchkey in the front door and placed his satchel down carefully on the floor. He sniffed. It was that kind of house.

Stale cigarettes, hamburgers and burnt toast. Nothing new, he knew what to expect. His mum was sprawled on the sofa, fast asleep. Daniel saw the sadness-lines around her mouth, and the parcel at her feet. Shiny pink material and tassels.

Shit! Dad would go ballistic. He was forever shouting at her about her addiction to buying clothes, which she never got round to wearing.

Daniel went to the kitchen and found his dinner - burnt sausages and mash, with peas floating in their yellow liquid. He threw the sausages and soggy peas away and put a fresh batch on the hob. While the water for the peas boiled he emptied the ashtray near his mother and took her parcel upstairs to hide in her wardrobe.

He looked at the clock. Dad would be home in half an hour. He ran to the sitting room and sprayed it with air freshener. Anything to take all those smells away. He rushed back and forth laying the table for three and grabbed a packet of crisps from the larder to keep him going until dinner.

Suddenly he had an urge to leave them to it. Catch the Circle Line to somewhere. He could go round and round till he knew where he wanted to go. But who would stop his dad when he lost it and smacked his mother's bewildered face? Wait till I get big, he thought. Bigger'n you.

Next morning, as he came down for school, his mother was at the fence talking to Sally next door. Nosy cow.

'I would leave him, but for the sake of Daniel,' he heard his mother say. You and me both, he thought, as he picked up his satchel and left for school.

There is a radio playing in a taxi

DANIEL MAITLAND

An extract from his new novella **Things Forgotten**

There is a radio playing in a taxi waiting outside the main entrance. It is playing a song none of them have ever heard. Despite their haste, they stop for a moment to listen. The song stops and the DJ announces in his everyminuteofeverydayisaparty voice, 'A blast from the past there folks! Where, I say; where are they now!' He sounds a horn, a mechanical voice sings a jingle, and three people move on, out of the rain and into the building - which has been painted. Yellow.

'Wha' gwan?'

But no-one answers, because they don't exactly know.

The nurse kisses her teeth in frustration, and says, 'This way,' heading straight through the open reception area and towards the lifts.

'Third flo,' she says as they get to the lifts. Somewhere a piano is playing - no, really.

There is a sign on the wall listing what happens where. It says 'Neonatal Ward: Fourth floor.'

The nurse kisses her teeth again and says something very rude in a voice that she hopes is too low for the children to hear, about no-one's mother in particular. Jenny and the boy smile at each other - that's a new one.

'Fourth flo,' she mutters, pressing the button a little too hard perhaps. And up they slide into the heart of the building. The piano dies away as the doors close... then starts again as they swish back open.

Nurse, shaking her head at the unlikely music, mutters an uncertain: 'This way...' And all are happy to see a sign indicating that she has at least got *that* right. The corridor they are walking along has a glass wall and they can see right down to the ground floor where the piano player is sitting at a big piano... uhm, playing it.

'That's pretty,' says Jenny, taking the boy's hand in a different way, and pulling him toward the edge to see. He smiles.

'Yes,' he says, looking down and then across at her. 'It is.'

The nurse refuses to look. And instead stamps on muttering, 'Ain' no batty boy piano-man... Ain no glass wall... Thought we was in uh urry.' And that bit about the mother, and how someone is 'gwan haff tell someone somethin real soon.' And kissing her teeth so fiercely that Jenny is worried she might suck them down her throat. She lets go of the boy's hand (thrilling at the loss) and catches up to the big lady ahead.

'You're smashing,' she says, giving the killer smile and replanting her hand somewhere useful.

'Hhmmm,' says the nurse, but her fingers are kind and soft around the little girl's. 'Thought we was in 'urry.'

'We are,' says Jenny. And then of course the worry creeps in. It does seem to have taken an awfully long time to get from the car park to here. How does one hurry from step to step, stone to stone, like this? There doesn't seem to be any way of speeding anything up - of jumping the whole pond to the other side, or doing without bloody ponds altogether. Just, you know, being there - now. She frowns. She feels heavy.

The boy catches up. 'Come on,' he says, and that at least is a comfort.

They pass a waiting area and it is filled up with people with messy hair in thin gowns that don't close properly. As always, there is a TV screen and they are all watching it. Jenny can almost see the grey images reflecting on their grey faces and she feels bad for them. She is hurrying, she remembers, must hurry past, stone to stone. But she can't, and stops - despite the mighty pull from the hand in which she is enfolded.

The Television is awful. Jenny had never seen it so awful. They are showing pictures of a war. Jenny didn't know there was a war.

'There's a war,' she breathes in horror.

The boy starts, 'Come on.' But then stops; also transfixed.

'Damn,' says the nurse.

People on the screen are actually shooting at each other, and hitting each other - in real life!! And they are in a really hot country and they are people that Jenny might know, that might live in her street. And they are shooting and being shot at by the people that live in the hot country - or who look like they probably do - they are wearing the right clothes; as opposed to the people from Jenny's street who are wearing big helmets and thick jackets, and must be melting inside like a sticky cake.

The Television moves to a hospital now. There is a room full of men with bits missing, and the Prince is shaking their hands while they smile bravely. And some of them are not smiling, but not shouting and punching the Prince either. Or saying, 'Why did I have to go and melt like a sticky cake and be blown up in someone else's street?'

'Come on,' says the nurse, pulling at the child. But the child won't move, she is shaking her head and crying for the broken men and for the ones about to be broken, and the ones being broken even now, at this very moment, on somebody else's street. The boy is shaking his head too and the man behind the desk is smiling at the camera and saying something about being a hero.

'Come on,' says the nurse. The TV reflectors have noticed the intruders and are moving their vacant eyes towards them.

'Come on,' says the nurse. But she is not pulling anymore, and it sounds more like an echo than a statement. And now the TV has changed and is instead showing an undersea picture of oil gushing from the floor of the world. And then it shows black birds that should have been all sorts of colours flapping weakly on beaches. And then it shows men in very nice suits smiling at an interviewer while they explain how they have been misunderstood. And then it shows the undersea black fountain again. And then it shows a black beach that should have been yellow. And then it shows sea lions and coral reefs. And then it shows the men. And then it changes again and people are sitting on top of roofs and brown water is drowning their houses and other people are carrying bundles over their heads and trying to wade through the brown water. And mothers are carrying naked babies in their arms. And the babies aren't moving. And the little girl has sat down on the floor. And the nurse is standing like a statue with tears pouring down her big brown cheeks. And the boy is standing beside the nurse. And all are transfixed by the screen; as black men in headscarves on horseback charge into a dirty campsite full of mothers and children waving swords and firing rifles.

The red number machine across the room beeps and changes to a new one. One of the reflectors coughs, and gets up and leaves. The nurse takes his seat - her eyes not leaving the screen for a second. The boy sits down on the floor next to the girl - more falls than sits actually - his eyes not leaving the screen for a second. Moscow is on fire and Russian people are hot and can't breathe. American people are dying too - of being very fat and unhappy... There is an advert...

The bald headed man with metal-rimmed glasses unplugs himself from the transmitter beside the desk - behind which the receptionist lies cold and unmoving. He places his claw hand back upon his lever and pushes right. The wheelchair whirs on its axis and heads back through the double doors - letting out a hint to the immobile watchers, not ten yards away, had they any attention left for such things, of what may or may not have been a scream.

There is a radio playing in a taxi

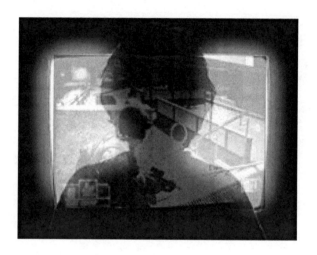

Alice

SUE JENNINGS

Alice walks towards the bus stop clutching her new, stripy plastic laundry bag. It is half-filled with washing. She has packed the washing liquid and the dosing ball she always uses because she likes to do this better than putting detergent into the two machine trays. She sees the monk out of the corner of her eye and her jaw tightens. His presence always worries her. His grey habit; his hands crossed before him, the rosary entwined in his fingers; his lowered head. All these evoke for Alice the convent school on penance afternoons. She turns her head and shoulders towards the shop side of the street.

The street smells of things dropped upon it and ground underfoot. Shops here are small and cluttered; few enjoy a brisk trade. There are tall Victorian houses; some well restored and renovated; some with rot rising from their disused basements, up the cracked and subsiding flights of stone steps and through the doors into the hallways.

Alice reaches the bus shelter. She can see that a small drama is playing there.

'Pick it up.'

A man holding a can of lager and accompanied by a broad-shouldered, toffee-coloured Staffordshire bull terrier jabs a finger at a young man dressed in shorts and a hoodie. Pale, dishevelled and sweating, the young man has dropped an empty drink carton and crisp-packet on the pavement near the shelter. Taking a swig of the lager, terrier-man twitches his green cotton jacket over his shoulder. His legs planted firmly two feet apart, head at an angle, unwavering eye contact; Alice stands close to the advertising panel, trying to be less of a spectator, a corkscrew of anxiety turning in her chest. She holds the bag of washing close to her body as though it were a child.

The young man presses the back of his hand to his lips. He bites his third finger.

'Street's dirty, man.'

Something like a roar begins in the dog-owner's chest. Before it is fully audible the hooded boy scoops up his litter and flees.

Terrier man crushes his empty can and impales it upon a nearby railing. Alice watches two flies as they circle in an upper corner of the bus shelter. She'd love to touch the dog, but doesn't dare.

Two tall African men in gleaming white robes stroll past the bus stop. Even now, a sense of *other* bewilders and agitates Alice.

The bus arrives.

The seats facing each other on the raised part of the bus are all occupied. Alice does not like to sit in the double seats further back. She dislikes being close to the backs of others' necks; she does not enjoy the sensation of strangers close behind her; worse still, she may become trapped by another passenger should she choose a window seat, or have to make the decision to sit next to someone who is already by a window. All the seats are taken by at least one passenger. Many are men.

Alice makes the only comfortable decision she can, and sits down next to a woman in white lace who clutches a bible and soft, white gloves. It is Sunday.

There are launderettes closer than the one to which Alice is going, but there are places she likes to see, to take stock of; those she has watched change over time, and those that don't change at all.

Now the bus is passing the cemetery and Alice gazes eagerly out of the window, for she can hear stories now, in her head; see, in the silent, backward tilt of the pale, stony sentinels, her own awe-filled anticipation of the release of waiting spirits.

Alice gets off the bus at the launderette. She loads the wash and wanders out; walks down the street to buy butterscotch. Under the bridge, the dark, dry September wind has lifted smells from the tiled corners beneath the subliminal promises of the hoardings. Alice stands sucking her sweets outside the apartment block that was once the convent school she'd attended. Briefly, she is twelve again, waiting for Moira, whom her mother mistrusts, and whose brother is an expert on all kinds of sex. Once, Alice remembers, she dreamt she had a penis. The dream did not distress her.

If it were not for the washing, she might walk home, as she had done so many times with Moira, or Gaya on Spring evenings after knockabout tennis on the school court. But it is not Spring now. Gaya is dead. Moira failed her O levels, and what she did after *that* rocked the whole school. All the more intriguing to the fifth years was the phrase used by Sister Marguerita: *gone to the dogs.* It was in the school hall during prayers for Moira's soul that Alice suddenly knew she had lost her own.

Alice collects the washing and boards the bus home.

Alice opens the door of her room. She is out of breath after climbing the forty-two stairs to the large, light room at the top of this Victorian house. She puts down her laundry bag, with its smell of warm washing, and moves toward the window. Looking out, she can see the park beyond the garden, its huge centrepiece an enormous oak tree where squirrels are seen attending to the business of food gathering. To the left lies the bowling-green; away to the right, the memorial gardens with their winding, concrete paths flanked by privet hedging. It is a peaceful, pleasant outlook.

Alice makes tea and sits in a wooden chair by the window. She has not always lived here, and sometimes she remembers the other places, although these memories have faded considerably of late. There are fewer people here. She leans her forearm on the window-sill. The radiator beneath hums quietly and emits a gentle heat, and Alice relaxes into the soft rhythm of its song. She feels happy.

There was a place once, Alice recalls, she visited, far from here, in the times when life was less structured: a steep, woodland track where several hundred feet of copper beeches were ranked on the descent, their bare branches forming a silvered cataract in the distance. Further along and farther down the gorge, leafless silver birch trees held aloft deep, lavender canopies; the colour had amazed and delighted her. Alice had talked there, on that day, for a long, long time. On rare days she still uses the language of that time, and speaks it to strangers. Because of its lyrical quality, and the eloquence of her eyes, she occasionally receives a response that pleases her. At these times, it does not matter so very much that she no longer has her soul; she has looked in so many places for it, she knows there are only a few left to search.

A noise startles Alice. On the lower landing, the girl who lives in the flat below arrives home, opens her door and calls to the cat. The door closes. Then, there is quiet, and all the sounds within it swirl around Alice's feet like a receding tide.

From a small bag she takes her prescription and counts out the evening dose. Today, she will wait for the light to fade before she swallows the pills. Taking her hat and coat from the peg, Alice descends the forty-two stairs to the street.

In these afternoon perambulations, Alice sometimes visits the places she knows she will walk as a ghost. She will be alone in the spirit world, and this causes her a moment's concern because her father and her brother will, of course, be walking around together. Then she brightens - a smile forms. As she steps into the empty lift in the shopping centre car park, she gives a little laugh:

The father, the son, and the lonely ghost.

As the lift doors open at ground level, shoppers step in: a young mother with a toddler in a trolley, an elderly couple with two carrier bags each, neither of them very full. Alice remains in the lift, returning to the car park. She repeats the journey up and down several times before she finally leaves the lift and walks down the hill, away from the shopping centre and towards the park.

Someone is shouting in the park. Alice cannot see who it is, but she can hear the remonstrative tone. A child begins to scream. Alice puts her hands over her ears, but she cannot shut the sound out. She cries out, softly at first, then more loudly, one repetitive utterance to call a halt, to shock into silence.

'Alice, Alice,' Mother would soothe, rocking the child. 'Alice…'

'ALICE!' There is a louder voice now. 'ALICE!'

Her cry becomes a keening; it is a song she has sung before and it completes her.

All that Alice has to do now is to capture her soul. She has seen it in the waters of the lake, but it is breaking up and floating away through the ripples. Holding it will be difficult because it is soft and shiny, and very heavy, but, she thinks, if she moves fast, she may be lucky.

There is a man by the lake. He is at some distance from the water, and he is looking towards Alice. She sees him raise an arm in a gesture, then cup both hands to his mouth. She lets her hands hang still at her sides. She has been trained to do this at the right times. Her hands are large. When she sees them reflected in the choppy, grey lake, she thinks they look like the hands of a cartoon character - and she smiles. As she enters the lake, she sees the man begin to move, fast, in her direction. She knows he is trying to help her somehow.

She feels a brief guilt about the tablets left on the table.

Gathering Myself

BECCA LEATHLEAN

Stood in the kitchen yesterday
sorting earrings into piles:
good
second-best
sentimental
charity.

Thirty years' life on the kitchen worktop:
a pair of Chinese charms,
hoops of plastic fruit,
copper flowers from Camberwell.
What happened to the girl who wore them?

Silver fish with tails like butchers' hooks;
turquoise and filigree from Montenegro.
From my cousin, a moonstone for Mum's funeral.
Red drops from Edinburgh,
gobby as boiled sweets.
A diaphanous butterfly wing in blue glass.

Traces of me
from quirky teen
to muted middle age.

This morning
I wore stripy earrings from Cornwall
and a splash of pearl pink lipstick
salvaged from the bin.

Without Parallel

RACHAEL DUNLOP

The kittens were sleeping under the workbench at the back of the garage. One grey, one black, they were curled together in a perfect circle, nose to tail, belly to belly, ying and yang. Hose in hand, Dave crouched down to look at them. He could turn the hose on them right now, but he was more inclined to pull out his phone and take a picture, they looked so cute. What was worse, he wondered, being cruel or being a wuss? Which was more of a weakness?

'C'mon, Dave. Bring that hose out here.'

Dave stood up with a sigh and went outside, pulling hard on the reluctant hose as he went. His twin brother Sam was inside the 4x4 car they were valeting, vacuuming the upholstery. It was the dog days of summer, and the seaside town where the boys lived was beginning to empty. They had set up their makeshift car wash in their parents' driveway and had done a roaring trade all summer, situated as they were on the main road in and out of town. Now people were bringing their cars in for a last clean up before the long drive home. The cars came in smelling of brine and fried food, with upholstery tacky with gum, and carpets granulated with sand. The twins worked the cars over with detergents and unguents until all traces of frivolity were gone.

Sam pulled his head out from the foot well where he had been vacuuming. 'Here's today's takings,' he said and handed Dave a soft wedge of folded five and ten pound notes. Dave liked it when the notes were well used and softened with age. They seemed to get stronger the more often they passed hands, unlike new notes that were crisp and stiff, but somehow brittle. Dave took the money and tucked it into his back pocket. Tomorrow he would bank it, along with the rest of the week's takings. The savings account was in both their names, but, of course, only one of them would be going to university in a few months time. They had turned eighteen in July. By the time university started in October it should be evident which one of them was going to survive.

Sam backed out of the car and turned off the vacuum. 'Mum called,' he said.

'Oh yeah?'

'Mandy Grey's dead.'

'Already?' Dave felt a rush of adrenaline flooding his muscles, his pulse beating hard against his throat, a sure sign of a panic attack coming on. He thought about the Grey twins, their next-door neighbours since they were all six years old. The four of them had been inseparable. Now there were three. Soon it would be two. Sam looked at him but said nothing. 'How was she...?' Dave couldn't finish the sentence.

'Eliminated? Leukaemia. Acute. She got an infection, so that speeded things along.'

Dave willed himself into calmness. 'How's Mum?'

'She's okay. She's glad we're both still here - for now.'

Dave envied his brother his sanguine outlook on their fate. Sam was cheerfully fatalistic and not given to thinking things through too much. Not like Dave. And it somehow didn't help to know that it happened to everyone: born in pairs, growing together, growing apart, only one allowed to reach adulthood. Dave and Sam were waiting for the genetic marker to kick in, decide which one of them would survive their nineteenth year.

Dave turned on the hose and played the water over the vehicle while his brother started sponging it down. 'I never thought Mandy would be the one to be eliminated,' he said. Sam snorted.

'Why, because she was the nice one? You don't still believe that good twin, evil twin mumbo-jumbo, do you? '

'Maybe if we knew how it worked...'

'Maybe we will, one day. Don't see how it would help, though. Can't change it.' Sam climbed back into the car to clean the dashboard.

Dave turned off the hose and picked up a sponge. Hunkering down to clean the hubcaps, he saw a pair of spiders busily casting a web in the wheel arches. He used the edge of his sponge to flick them out. An insect's life was so short, it hardly seemed worth having them born in pairs too. But there it was - Mother Nature knew best.

Can't change it. His brother's words echoed around Dave's head. What if that weren't true? What if one of them was to die before the elimination? Not by accident or illness, but killed. Murdered. Dave knew all the arguments against that. The surviving twin was always the chief suspect. If you were convicted, and you weren't eliminated naturally, they handed you over to the executioners. Either way, you died. It wouldn't have been worth the risk, if your chances of being eliminated were still fifty-fifty. But that was the great anomaly, the fact that geneticists, mathematicians and moralists all over the world were trying to explain - if your twin died before elimination, your chances of survival were better than fifty-fifty. Only by a fraction of a percent, but still better.

Dave picked up a brush and started scrubbing the wheels. Sea salt and black brake fluid had been baked together into an immoveable compound that resisted everything but pure elbow grease. This was why the boys had done so well this summer with their car wash - attention to detail. Dave let the rhythmical movement of his arm calm his brain. Thinking about this was getting him nowhere - the snake of logic was swallowing its own tail, and choking on it.

'Dave, are you finished yet? Mr Barrows is going pick his car up tomorrow, so we should put it in the garage overnight.'

'Yeah, I'm finished. Let me just chase those kittens out before you back it in.'

Dave ducked his head under the workbench. 'Aw, no.'

The grey kitten was still lying down, one curlicue half of a circle that was now broken. The black kitten stood over the grey one, nudging him with his nose, not yet realising his brother was dead. Dave scooped the black kitten up in his hand. 'Guess you were the lucky one,' he said. He didn't see the gleaming 4x4 reversing towards him. Reversing and picking up speed.

New York Streets

MARTI MIRKIN

In a cafe on the corner
    of West Houston and Broadway

It is Big Apple hot and it's El Nino sunny
    and I'm looking for a lover
    to share
    my
    ice-cold
    marguarita.

God - but New York men look -
    good-

        after twenty years in England
        even the bad ones look -
        good -

        even the old ones
        with their roll of fat
        and walking sticks -
        don't look bad !

It's how they walk,
    how their feet
    meet the street -

confident tigers
    in free-wheeling camouflage
    and rhythm -
Yes,
New Yorkers are good walkers,

    It's a love affair with the sidewalks
    and I want to join.

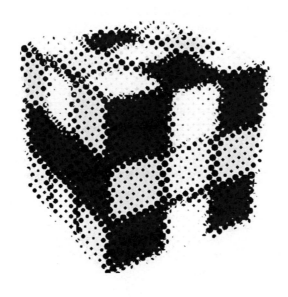

High Definition New Year

EMMA MACKINNON

Janine's kitchen reflected the chaotic contents of her head. Her inner dirty dishes, the half-dried laundry. Smears of sticky stuff, crumbs and piles of paper. Drawers full of dried up felt tips, unknown bunches of keys and Christmas cards from three years ago. A long defunct food mixer. How could it be so hard to get a room to make sense?

Outside, a crust of snow reflected blue sky. So Janine put on sunglasses. Walking in the park in the clarity of ice and sharp light to try and start again. This time she wouldn't let things build up. Work things. Home things. So many mini scenarios. Fractured glimpses of faces. Of conversations, meetings and memos - and always scrappy lists of jobs to do. She would begin with a pared down mind. A cool, kind, white painted Swedish one with empty surfaces on which to rest her elbows, head bowed, always so tired. She would sort her thoughts into neat labelled piles and maybe even throw out those she didn't want in the process. If only she could slow down enough to do it. If only she could stop.

It was teatime then - and the curtains that Janine had made a resolution to wash hung shroud-like on the line outside. Stiffening in the first evening of the New Year.

'I can't come to it, Ella - you know I can never come to those things, but I'll be thinking of you, you know I will ... and you'll be great.'

Janine knelt down. Her features, a baggier, disappointed version of her daughter's. But Ella shrugged away, slowly forking in pasta at the small messy table.

'They said bring my costume in tomorrow. I have to or they said I couldn't be in it. My teacher said I had to wear all green.'

Trouble

Ella was hungry. Of course she'd had breakfast. She didn't have a bad mum. But the Rice Krispies had been eaten when it was nearly still night. In the freezing gloom before birdsong. And she'd struggled to school, with her packed lunch and her PE kit and her show-and-tell Spanish doll and the outfit for the assembly that, well, wasn't really green, more patterny - and which was her summer dress from last year together with some turquoise socks of Janine's. Janine hadn't meant to shout the night before but it had got so late.

'Why are you telling me this now when you've had the whole holiday? I think you do it on purpose. You're trouble. Always causing trouble,' she'd accused, stabbing an aspirin from it's plastic.

'Just go to bed,' she'd snapped at her daughter. 'Just go away and give me some peace.'

When Ella went to her friends' homes, not often because of after school club but sometimes in the holidays, it was different. Nothing she could really identify. Perhaps the colours were bolder or the edges of furniture more defined. There were rules but no-one shouted. And there were always people around who didn't have to be busy all the time and could spend ages showing her the pet rabbits. She didn't have to hide when the doorbell rang, as she did when she'd been left at home on a Saturday. Alone, dull and anxious.

Once in the past Janine had been a lot more pleased with herself. She'd been able to call herself an actor. Fringe, and then a career apparently sealed by odd appearances in television soaps. A soap in itself, the relationship that began in the make-up trailer with Jack had ended shortly after Ella was born. Janine enjoyed pregnancy but was astonished at its cost of both partner and career.

Deep in his new wasted nocturnal parenting role, Jack had grown Edwardian whiskers. In a crumpled white shirt he'd draped himself confidentially over childless friends:

'It's such an amazing experience man - I can't tell you.' But at a party, people drawn briefly to the couple's bundle had quickly lost interest.

'Sorry, love - must just catch Charlotte.' Jack also found he needed to catch Charlotte. And her firm stomach and uninterrupted bed. Janine's life shrank away.

The family members who'd shown some interest lived in Scotland. Too far to be useful. Soon Janine found herself with a pack of economy custard creams and some nappy coupons. Watching with curiosity, on TV, the people who had once been her colleagues. So she'd been grateful for the interview and offer (though there was no part time option) and tried to do her best. Doing an okay office job. *Don't give up the day job*. Doing a job that was finding work for other actors.

Orange Patent Platforms

And now it was time for break in the overheated classroom with chewing gum stuck on the ancient radiators and high up Victorian windows carelessly painted shut. Ella wasted half an hour looking for a rubber then sharpened her pencil to a stub. She sat with her hands over her ears. She didn't have to write.

'You have to write something' Alfie said. 'You only done the date. Look at mine. I done mine. I done all this.'
Ella glanced at the page of scribble. 'Shut up. I don't care. It's nearly playtime. I don't have to write.'

'And Ella - if you can't work during the lesson you can do it in your own time.'

Ella flinched as her name was flung at her like a shoe. Like one of Miss Hebden's orange patent platforms. Miss Alicia Hebden lurched over her. Huge as a bear.

'I want that finished by the end of play or I'll be speaking to your parents.'

Parent. Ella thought of Janine's skin, the makeup applied and forgotten, smudged greasily into the creases of her forehead. She smiled to stop the tears coming.

'Right young lady, you'll be telling the Headteacher why you think it's so funny to miss your free time.' Miss Hebden held up Ella's book, exposing its blankness. There were giggles and whispers.

'This is not what I expect from anyone in my class. Take this to Miss Crewe's office. I want to see at least a page of writing by the time the bell goes. The rest of you - line up for assembly.'

There were only two small peaks in Ella's day. One was the story before home time when she could lose herself in the plot of *Horrid Henry*. The other was when she saw the brown shape of her mum's coat behind the frosted glass of the community centre door at six o'clock.

Heat and Serve

Janine parked badly. She would be only three minutes late, but she would have to pay for a further fifteen. Stuck behind a number 12 bus. Time ticking away. Again she felt distanced from the cosy perfection she perceived other peoples lives to be, but her automatic acting skills kicked in as she reached the building. An apologetic smile.

'I am SO sorry. Traffic's mad this evening. Come on darling, let's get you home.' Behind them a couple of dumpy women in overalls cleared the hall:

'...and she can't even get here on time. Smell the drink on 'er a mile off.'

The curtains were about the only reasonably wholesome items in Janine's kitchen she decided, once home. Grime blurred her vision. Worktops were disguised by empty take away containers and cups containing floating islands of mould. A dull fur of dust lay on the shelves. It reminded Janine that she should do something, but she couldn't remember what.

'I'm going to lie down for a while,' she told Ella. By midnight they'd swallowed a desiccated arrangement of nuggets and pizza. From freezer to microwave to mouth. Janine lay on the sofa in her work clothes, a sickly TV flicker playing over her unconscious body. But Ella had dragged herself upstairs and lay thinking of the school assembly. It didn't matter what she'd worn or even that Janine had failed to attend. On that stage, a disco ball had whirled in Ella's head.

Full Stops

At eight thirty in the morning Alicia Hebden had been busy at work for an hour. A cup of instant and a bag of crisps served to focus her thoughts on marking twenty-eight English books. All pretty similar. Each following a prescribed formula that allowed little opportunity for real expression. At least they'd done the work. Alicia, energised by the fact that she wouldn't have to squeeze the dregs from a topic they'd lost interest in three weeks ago, felt her stress levels drop. The Head would be pleased. Most of the children had used rulers to underline and they'd remembered their full stops. The only thing left to do was to add a pertinent yet encouraging comment and slap on a few smiley stickers, knowing the literacy coordinator would be checking the books later.

The last one in the pile was Ella's. Alicia scowled through her Top Shop tortoiseshells. Yesterday's date had been carefully scribed, but that was all. On the opposite page Ella had drawn a face. Scrawled in dark angry pencil, ripping through the paper in places - it filled the entire area. Ella had coloured the mouth in bright red and it was full of jagged, feline looking teeth.

Sometimes Alicia enjoyed teaching. When her routine went smoothly. When tension didn't make her squawk instructions. She spoke. She explained. They went to their tables and did as she had asked. She managed a nice filter coffee at break and had time for lunch. All things that required minimal personal involvement. She had a flat, a shiny little car and an engagement ring. The world was a simple, colourful puzzle she thought she could solve. But today was not going according to plan. She had to sneak a chocolate bar from her drawer, she felt so sour.

'I don't understand,' she wailed to Carol, the Learning Mentor. 'She knows how to do it but she won't - then this.'

'Have you noticed,' Carol observed, 'the mum's not been to any of the parents evenings. It might be an idea to arrange a meeting.'

Alicia raked pearly nails through her hairstyle. Annoyed that she'd been asked to intervene in the life of this eccentric child and her absent mother.

'I'll do it this week.' She thought: *Yeah - if I can fit it in between Rod's birthday and Friday's so-called team building event.*

Road Kill

On a day when buildings were stacked one in front of another like monumental cereal packets full of people at futile tasks, Janine knew civilisation had reached its zenith and was falling fast. A man propped his vested belly on a sill, dragging on a cigarette. Youths. Laughing, hawking. Spitting on a pigeon's back, turning up their headphones treble....

Janine's movements, as if on a conveyor belt took her past a girl gang of giant teenagers cramming hamburgers. Shrieking. Decaying shop fronts repeated themselves, endlessly mirrored into the horizon. A dead cat lay on the pavement, eyeballs knocked out like bloody marbles. Traffic pounded against bruised tarmac.

Part of Janine shrivelled up and blew down the street. Kicking along - with all the other old crisp packets and used fast food wrappings.

Play To Your Strengths

Janine said across the barrier of a school table:

'Yes. I do reading with her when I can. I work long hours. It's just me. I'm on my own. We try but there's not much time left after tea for homework. I'm sorry. I don't know why she did that picture. I've never seen anything like it before. I'm sorry she spoilt her book.'

'It's okay. It must be difficult for you both.' Alicia struggled to keep a professionally sympathetic eye contact. They'd gone way over time. Adults coughed and shuffled outside the classroom. A toddler was rattling the door handle.

'Maybe she could have a friend over at the weekend. They could do homework - and play too?' It was what Carol had told Alicia to say.

'I could.... do that.' Janine said slowly.

Janine looked unusual, Alicia thought. Unwell. Her eyes glittering, the sockets purple and lined. Her skin yellow. Though she was smartly dressed in a dark neutral outfit, the clothes looked like a uniform, as if she had no desire to express herself through them. She had been staring at Alicia too long.

'Good. Great. Let me know how that goes then.'

Alicia slid her gaze to the clock. Standing, she shuffled papers towards Janine signalling the end of the session. 'So. Lovely to meet you. You can make an appointment to see me any time...'

'It's not real you know.'

'Scuse me?' Alicia frowned. *What now for crying out loud?*

'All this is just molecules. It looks like things but it's nothing.' Janine explained patiently.

Great. Alicia gritted her teeth.

'It's nothing - but it's matter. It's matter but it's nothing. Nothing matters. All these molecules are mostly nothing. So what's the point of anything? Do you understand? We are nothing and this world is an illusion.' Janine was not even looking at Alicia now, but through her and she stretched out her hands as if she were blind.

The stuff of life as Janine saw it was disintegrating. Breaking down into individual shimmering particles that ran through and into her fingers. Like an ancient city in a sandstorm, the classroom dissolved in an iridescent drift.

Alicia stepped back awkwardly into a filing cabinet, sending a Rubik's Cube clattering to the floor. Usually she experienced parents as some sort of malevolent breed. Demanding and griping. Either hot-housing their offspring or beating them black and blue. Leaving her to repair the damage as well as teach. But Janine fitted none of these categories. The woman was ill, surely. Ill or drunk. Or drugged. She was also rather scary, sitting there palms up, feeling something Alicia couldn't see.

'Are you all right?' asked Alicia finally. It was best to be direct: 'Have you been drinking?'

'No. I've been thinking.' Janine sounded remote.

'What is it?' Alicia hesitated. 'What's.... out there?'

'I'm part of it. We are all part of it.' Janine unable to express her deconstructed vision, looked beyond the room, forming a circle with her arms. 'We're all part of nothing.'

Alicia thought quickly in textbook idioms. *Maintain the channels of communication. Focus.*

'Well. Ella isn't nothing. She's actually quite something,' she rattled. 'She was brilliant in our assembly. She really sparkled. Quite different from how she is in class. Totally amazed us. I expect she gets it from you. You know - I think she has natural talent.'

Janine had turned her unblinking face to Alicia.

'You don't have to go there, Janine,' Alicia said. 'You've got to stop. It's time to wake up. You have to come back. For Ella.'

'For Ella,' Janine repeated in a monotone.

'Yes - she needs you.'

'I didn't... know. I've been... I'm so tired...'

Instinctively Alicia moved next to Janine. They crouched together on the child-sized chairs.

'We can get you some help. Come on, Janine. The show must go on.'

'Must it?'

'Yes,' said Alicia firmly 'It must.'

After Janine had been escorted, still sobbing, from the Head's office into the back of an ambulance parked discreetly at the side entrance to the school, Alicia found the number of an old friend. Someone she'd lost touch with when her own career lurched from theatre to teaching. Film producer and casting director, Sam Springett.

Funny You Should Say That...

'Why did you do it?' Rod questioned Alicia over the hiss of the stir-fry. 'Why was it any of your business? They work you hard enough in that place as it is. Supposing Sam doesn't want her for the role. Woman sounds as if she needs medication - not a bloody job. Have we got any soy sauce?'

'Because I had to. I never realised. But seeing how people can help themselves - I think it's what I'm best at. Apart from shopping.' Alicia glanced slyly at Rod. 'Anyway - if she gets the part, it *will* be a kind of medication.'

'If!' Rod was scornful. 'You'll be giving up teaching to become a shrink next. Do you want noodles or rice?'

Important Objects

The lack of furniture made Janine's voice echo up the stairwell.

'Are you ready, Ells?'

The important objects of the last decade stood in the living room, condensed into a few cardboard boxes. Her life with Ella trussed up and ready to go. A satisfying beige emptiness inhabited the house. It was chilly with the front door open. *That's that then.* Janine ran a cloth along the windowsill. 'What are you doing mum?' Ella appeared, wearing her coat and rucksack.

'Leaving it clean for the new people. I wouldn't want to move into somewhere dirty.'

'It would be yucky,' agreed Ella.

Janine checked her watch and felt the weight of her new holdall. Made of quality leather, it boasted *S.S. Productions Inc* in confident puce along one side.

'Mum - when I go to my new school do I get to do acting all the time?'

'Not quite.' Janine was smiling. 'But more than at St Luke's.'

They heard the robot voice of a lorry reversing outside...

'Haven't packed the kettle yet have you?' the men joked. 'And what about them? You taking those?'

'No.' Janine walked to the window. 'No we're not taking these. They're staying.' And she pulled the kitchen curtains wide open, letting in the new spring sun.

Loss

SUE JENNINGS

The note said: *Gone Home.*
I did not see when she jumped,
but I'd heard her say:

'I am displaced', and
often, upon waking, she
would tell of her home.

Tell how she'd wander
through each room in her night dreams;
how, an age away,

the rooms stayed the same,
each creaking board remembered,
each door open, still.

Before the leaping,
I had not known her for long:
but she was fading

like purple heather
in the last days of summer
before the fall.

The End

MARK KIELY

She was like Christmas. Simply being with her filled me with joy. It was April, and yet the melodies of festive carols echoed around us. The ghosts of young children gathered at the far end of the platform, invisible to her eyes in the afternoon's eager sunshine. They were singing like angels, snow already beginning to cover their footprints.

'I feel cheated if an opera has a happy ending.'

I raised my hands in a gesture of deferral. 'It might have a happy ending, but, for me, it's still very poignant. You'll be in tears long before the finale.'

'When the slave-girl sacrifices herself for the man she forlornly loves?'

The slave-girl's name was Liu. 'Trust me. By the time we're home tonight, it will be your favourite opera too.'

The train appeared in the distance, slowly growing in size as it approached the station. When I was seven years old, Christmas had been an expensive train-set. 'Here it comes. I said we'd have time for a pizza.'

'And a bottle of wine?'

'Each.'

A smile of innocent mischievousness spread across her face. There was nothing I found more irresistible about her, and I could have dropped to my knees right there, in full view of the driver on the approaching train, and begged her to make love to me. Wild, honest, gentle love.

Two minutes later, sitting opposite each other on the train, we were both absorbed in magazine articles to an extent that precluded virtually all awareness of the other's presence. Six months earlier, this had been one of our first understandings. We would feel no compulsion to make conversation when journeying on public transport. It was an early piece of common ground - this realisation that we shared a fear of being trapped in situations where we were compelled to communicate. Her other great fear, of confined spaces, together with my vaguely ideological unease with cars, meant that a good deal of our time together was spent not communicating on trains and buses. Perhaps the space this allowed us helped to cement our partnership.

We went for a pizza and a bottle of wine in our favourite restaurant in Soho, enjoyed the opera, drank another bottle of wine, went back to her flat on a night-bus, had sex, and practised a little Arabic for our forthcoming trip to Morocco. Before falling asleep.

It was Christmas morning, yet colder, darker, lonelier. I was naked and child-like, stumbling from her flat into my parents' house. Like an imaginary sister, my girlfriend had disappeared, and, despite my fear, I could not stop my feet. They were taking me where I did not wish to go. The door was ahead of me. It was closed, but I knew what was inside. I did not want to see it again. I did not want to be back here. With a soundless cry and considerable relief, I awoke.

'Not again! What is wrong with you?' Shock, disgust, concern, even fear were there in her eyes. There was no room left to hold in the tears that traced delicate paths along her cheeks.

It was Sunday morning, and she did not have to go to work. Walking into the bathroom with a full bladder - before falling asleep we had shared a bottle of mineral water - she found me standing naked at the sink. My hands were covered with blood, and yet I still carried on scrubbing at them.

I looked at her and then looked back down. What on earth was I doing? There was no longer any lather from the soap. I was not even rubbing anymore. I was scratching. Oh my God. Am I mad?

This was not the first time she had seen me like this after we made love. The previous occasion had been shortly after we first met. It had been one of the most wonderful nights of my life, and then, just like this morning, she had found me like this. I had cried, and she had cried, and then we cradled each other as if to convince ourselves that it was nothing more than a momentary bad dream. Now it was just her crying. I tried to tell her about bacteria, viruses, odours, shit. Hands got everywhere, touched everything. Reaching hesitantly under a rock, I felt the sting of a scorpion, and then I fell asleep. Back in the bathroom, naked and with speckles of blood on my body, I realised that she did not understand my words. The opera had been sung in Italian, and neither of us could make out Princess Turandot's eulogising of how fire could melt the ice encasing her own heart. Nevertheless, we both understood. Sitting there together. Holding hands. Now she did not understand.

Sitting at opposite ends of the sofa a short while later, when she asked me if it was her and did she disgust me in some way, I wanted to reach out and hug her. But my hands were bandaged and covered in ointment. When they were wrapped like this, they could not touch her in the way that we had touched and explored each other's bodies last night, and they could not leave me with the bottomless desire to clean them. But neither could they hold onto her.

That night I was back there. Trekking remorselessly the distance from her bedroom back to my parents'. The door was still closed, but I could open it. I had to open it, although nothing within me wanted to look inside. I touched the handle - I was lying beside her, giggling amid the mess of a tangled duvet, sharing a slice of toast and marmite, listening to a late-night phone-in show - *and slowly pushed. I wanted to remain with her, but, more than this, I wanted to lose her.*

I stepped into the room. They were still there. The two of them. They were just as I remembered. The sheets and blankets were smooth, uncreased, tucked neatly beneath the mattress. Tonight, as every night, she lay on her side facing me, eyes closed with lack of interest. He was on his back, snoring noisily up towards God. They looked like they had never touched each other in their lives.

Biographies

Fabian Acker has won a number of short story competitions, as well as the Travel Writer of The Year Award from the *Sunday Times*, the BT Technology Writer of the Year, and used to contribute regularly to Radio 4's travel programme, *Itchy Feet*. The first third of his working life he spent as a merchant seaman (except for two years military service in the Royal Engineers), the second third as a journalist, and he is now working his way through the last third under the motto *Don't Stop Breathing*. He is a Bargee First Class, and claims to have once been a bus conductor for Huddersfield Transport Corporation. He works occasionally for the National Council of Journalists as a tutor, trying to discourage journalists from using clichés, but without much light at the end of the tunnel.

Debi Alper has been a member of the East Dulwich Writers' Group since the last millennium. She has completed five novels in the Nirvana series of thrillers set in South East London. The first two, ***Nirvana Bites*** and ***Trading Tatiana***, have been published by Orion. 2010 has been a very busy year for Debi. She ran courses at the Festival of Writing in York, was a judge for the inaugural Brit Writers' Awards (novels category), has hosted workshops, edited manuscripts, mentored authors, and has had a short story published in *33*, an anthology with a story set in each of London's boroughs (published by Glasshouse Books). She often wishes she had more time to spend on her own writing. She also often wishes she was saner, but suspects she'd find that boring.
Debi's website is www.debialper.co.uk
She blogs at http://debialper.blogspot.com

Biographies

Joanna Czechowska, who joined the East Dulwich Writers' Group in 2007, is a journalist at a well-known women's magazine. She has written short stories for publications such as Best, The Lady, That's Life and Woman. Her debut novel, *The Black Madonna of Derby*, published by Silkmill Press at £7.99, came out in 2008 and draws on her early experiences of life with a Polish father and growing up in the immigrant Polish community in Derby. The sequel to this novel is in the works.
www.jczechowska.com

Rachael Dunlop is a writer of short stories and the blog *Butterflies*. She was the winner of the NYC Midnight Creative Writing Championships in 2009 and her story *Holding Patterns* was published in *33*, an anthology of short stories set in each of the London boroughs (Glasshouse Books, 2010). She has been working on her first novel for the past year with little discernible progress. She lives in a very big house in South East London but has yet to find a room of her own.
http://rachaeldunlop.blogspot.com/

Amy Griggs is a magazine editor, but enjoys writing stories for children and adults in her spare time. She lives in Crystal Palace and is a fan of cats, cricket and crazy Swedes.

Biographies

Galatia Grigoraki is the name under which Galatia Poli-topoulou, Neuroscientist, Stem Cell Biologist and poet par excellence, publishes, or hopes to, fictional things, as opposed to hard science... She lives in London most of the time although Greek childhood and roots and an insatiable taste for travel and unknown cultures, disrupt that living from time to time, often for years at a time. In fact she may eventually move back South, to a place where October and November are still fairly dry and sunny, and by April Fools' Day it is definitely spring!

Helen Hardy has been writing since she could hold a pen, starting with extensive disquisitions on chocolate moose, mouse and muse. By the time she learned to spell mousse, she knew that words were fascinating and serendipitous things. Helen was recent-ly a Brit Writers' Awards winner for her short story *Crush*. With the invaluable support of the East Dulwich Writer's Group she has also ventured into longer fiction, writing her first novel *Mother of the World*, set in Cairo during the Second World War. Helen lives in Norwood and is now researching a future novel inspired by the area's history.

Sue Jennings' contributions to this book deal with the sub-ject of the emotional struggle some people have with London life. Having returned to, and made her peace with the city of her birth, she continues to seek the pagan renewal of tidal water by rowing a small boat around the creeks of the river Medway. Sue continues to write, having not yet encountered discouragement strong enough to prevent her from doing so. Oh, well...

Biographies

Mark Kiely works as an acupuncturist in East Dulwich and likes to travel the world when the opportunity presents itself. Having submitted a story with an irrepressibly upbeat ending to the first *Hoovering the Roof* collection, he has enjoyed exploring some darker themes in the stories in this anthology.

Sue Lanzon spent twenty years as a photographer and illustrator, working on editorial and advertising accounts and exhibiting her personal work both in the U.K. and abroad. She qualified as a homeopath in 1998 and has a private practice in South London. She also teaches relaxation and meditation. Sue started writing about homeopathy in response to the current campaign to discredit it in the U.K. For homeopathic enquiries and/or publishing contracts, please contact Sue at suelanzminnie@btinternet.com

Becca Leathlean is a former journalist who has spent the last year setting up Alhambra, a Spanish-themed shop and arts cafe in Sydenham selling homeware and gifts and serving tapas. It's been rather full-on so she hasn't had as much time to write as she would have liked. *Gathering Myself* and *Formative Friendships* were both written soon after moving home a few years ago and re-edited for inclusion in *Hoovering the Roof 2*. Next year, Becca intends to make time to get inspired and write something new!

Biographies

Barbara Lovett recently finished an MA in Creative Writing at City University and works as a freelance writer, journalist and translator for various websites. Published work includes articles about self-made millionaires, musical stars and foot fetishists for Austrian and German magazines such as *Gewinn, Wienerin, Bühne* and *Orpheus*. Her play, *Tosca Mortale*, was published by Theater-verlag Bunte Bühne, Vienna. Barbara wants to thank everybody at EDWG for their input and help even though she always reads out her writing viz a funny akzent.

Lynsay Mackay began writing fan fiction in the Highlands, where she was born. Soon the constraints of another's work and rules proved too tight a net and she began to do her own thing. When not writing she can be found touring the streets of London on bike or trying to work out how to get together enough money for her next big adventure. As a life long fantasy fan she hopes her first novel will be in that genre but having just discovered a passion for short stories and non-fiction anything could happen.

Daniel Maitland having spent the majority of his adult life writing two novels, a poetry anthology, an album and a number of 'to do' lists, and with a pension crisis looming, Mr Maitland is now focussing on the much more realistic goals of winning the World Series Of Poker, and becoming the first person to qualify for the European Golf senior tour without ever having played professionally.

Emma MacKinnon
Goes to school.
Comes home. Cooks tea.
Writes and paints.
Gets on with stuff
Doesn't get on with stuff.
Likes a bit of rock 'n' roll.
(Has been close to going to work in slippers - but so far common sense has prevailed.)

Maxine McLeary-Jones is a multitasking working wife
and mother with a passion for writing. From an early age she would write fairy tales and read them to her siblings. Maxine holds an honours degree in English and has dabbled in journalism. She currently works in Government communications.

Ferdi Mehmet is an active member of The East Dulwich
Writers' Group. He writes novels, short stories, screenplays, and poetry. He enjoys various types of books (fictional, educational, comic books), films, and music. Ferdi has interests in psychology, human nature, and existentialism. His literary influences include Hunter S. Thompson and Elmore Leonard. Ferdi is a Priest of Dudeism (also known as The Church of the Latter-Day Dude), a growing, worldwide religion inspired by the character 'The Dude' from the 1998 film *The Big Lebowski*.

Biographies

Marti Mirkin is still looking for the next turning in the road, meeting many good people along the way. Walking very slowly is no disadvantage, especially near the ocean.

Anand Nair worked for the British Council in many African countries for fifteen years. In her other life she used to be a Mathematics teacher and has co-authored, *Mathematics Methods for Primary Teachers* (Macmillan, 1991), with a colleague. Her first novel, A *Streak of Sandalwood*, set in Kerala, India, was published by Authorhouse in 2009. She is currently writing her second novel, *Miles to Go*, set in wartime Kerala. She is a keen gardener and when the muse fails her, there is the garden for sustenance.

Kate Rose has a First Class degree from King's College and an MA in Creative Writing from Goldsmiths University. She has previously published a short story in the Goldfish Anthology. She has written freelance for various publications and published a medical book in the U.S.A. Kate's novel in progress, *The Hidden Phases of Venus* is set in Sydenham and spans the 1860s to present day. It explores the quests of two women as they attempt to reconcile freedom, love and art.

Biographies

Baruch Solomon is better known to residents of Dulwich as 'Barry the Gardener' or 'That nice young man who cuts my grass once a fortnight.' He has experimented with a variety of writing genres and finds short stories to be the most rewarding. 'With a short story, it's possible to use brevity to generate suggestion, ambiguity and a little bit of magic.' When not pulling out bindweed or writing for 'Hoovering the Roof', Baruch enjoys travel, voluntary work and 'putting the world to rights' over a few beers.

Emily Wiffen has an Oxford philosophy degree, which she thinks explains a lot. She has variously been a secretary, a teacher, a school librarian and other sundry things, some more interesting than others. After ten years of nomadically moving round the country she settled in East Dulwich and now shares a flat with some fluffy toys, some overdue library books, an overworked laptop and a drawer full of unfinished novels. She is writing this on the back of an envelope.

Richard Woodhouse's first novel, *Deathless,* a ghost story set in a limbo London, is available from **lulu.com**. A second novel, *Mr. Reed*, about a man who is too good to be true, is not available anywhere - because he is still writing it.
Website: **rhkw.co.uk**.

EAST DULWICH WRITERS' GROUP

edwg.co.uk

earwig press
2010